Love Triangle

Sylvia Morrow

Copyright © 2023 by Sylvia Morrow

All rights reserved.

No portion of this book may be reproduced in any form without written permission from the publisher or author, except as permitted by U.S. copyright law.

The author is against generative AI in its current unethical state. No part of this work may be used to train AI or uploaded to AI in any way.

Cover art by Latrexa Nova, Unfortunate Reads, and Duff, with additional Canva assets.

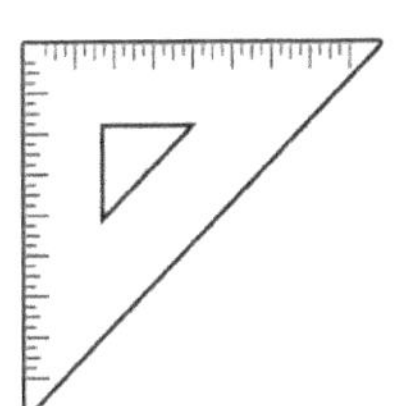

Content Considerations

This book is about an MMF, polyamorous relationship. There are moments of internalized biphobia, and times when characters may not believe a polyam relationship is possible, but the author promises a happy ending for all three main characters.

There may be triggers in this book for some people related to sex, injury, violent speech, or other topics. If you are concerned about a possible issue with content, please see the Sylvia Morrow website for a list of triggers. You may also contact Sylvia Morrow directly with questions.

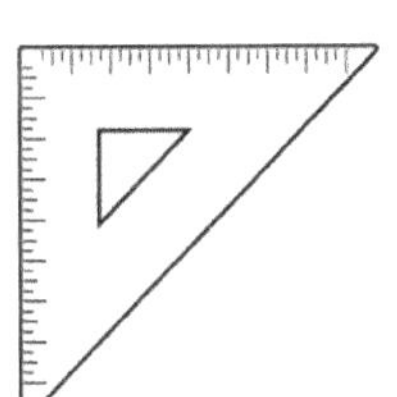

Chapter One
Cliff

T he scent of the air taunts me, a reminder of my failure to be on time. Normally, I take my lunch at exactly eleven a.m. I like to be punctual. Today, however, I needed to go home and shower after processing a particularly dirty new display piece for the museum. Now it's after twelve, and the mornings-only café where I eat every day is closed. *Damn.* Still able to smell the bacon sandwiches I order every day, I watch the light traffic on Main Street. Our town, Isawsa Falls, named after the great war hero Isawsa Lee, is small. We only have the one truly busy road, with the museum on one end, the high school on the other, and the quiet highway going straight down the middle.

The Isawsa Lee Foundation Museum, where I am in charge of everything geology-related, is the real local draw. The money made from the tourists visiting the ILFM keeps this town alive. I don't have time to waste standing here doing nothing, but when my routine is thrown off, I get a bit...lost. I'm not great with change, to put it lightly.

I shuffle nervously in place as I look around at the people going about their day. The weather today is unseasonably warm, so there are plenty of people out and about. Mothers walk their small children in strollers. Old men sit on benches arguing about local politics. A beautiful woman with icy blonde hair hangs a sign in a shop window.

Wait. I've never seen that woman before. And that building was the old boot shop that closed months ago. I noticed the "For Sale" signs had been removed but I didn't think anything new had been set up yet. *It seems someone was busy behind those brick walls.*

The woman steps back, placing her hands on her wide hips, and looks up at the sign to check her work. She readjusts it just slightly and looks over it once more. With a satisfied nod, she steps away and walks inside the brick building.

Crystal's Pies
Now Open

The sign sparkles in glittering rainbow letters. Pie. *Hmm.* Not the healthiest lunch, but it's open and I'm hungry.

What if it's bad?

My anxiety over any unexpected change doesn't want me to dine there.

You can wait until you get home, then have your regular, safe food.

I frown at the thought of another night of canned soup and toast, but I know that it's safe and reliable, at least.

But did you see how beautiful she was?

My libido chimes in. I thought the damn thing was dead, considering how uninterested in sex I've been lately.

Why don't you go get a taste of her pie? Well, this is an interesting turn of events. As much as I prefer to play things safe, I don't think I can resist listening to my...*heart*...the one time it speaks up in forever.

That decides it. I cross the street and head toward the new shop.

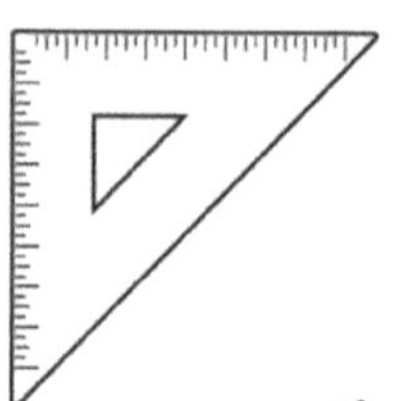

Chapter Two
Trig

A *h, dang.* Late for lunch again. Every other day this happens. The students turn their papers in at eleven, I look them over, and next thing I know my lunch time has come and gone.

Well, at least I'm only a little late this time. My lunch break is supposed to be from eleven fifty a.m. to twelve forty p.m., but it's just after noon right now. No time to grab anything last minute at the café, but I can grab a candy bar at the gas station. Something to fuel me until the end of the work day.

I wipe my glasses off on the hem of my button-down shirt (which is admittedly more wrinkled than I thought, oops) and put them back on. I start to leave but turn back when I realize I forgot my wallet and phone. Once I get them, I finally head out.

It's really nice weather and everyone outside is smiling and happy as heck. Everyone except Cliff from the museum. He's standing a ways ahead of me on the street looking like he's freaking out inside or something. He's all sweaty and his fists are clenched at his sides and, I don't know, he just looks stressed out. He's never exactly the smiling happy type, but he looks like crap right now.

I debate for a second whether or not to go talk to him to see if he needs help. As a teacher I spend all day helping people, it's what I was meant to do, and if he needs it and I don't offer it I would just feel terrible. But on the other hand, he's a prick and I don't want him to be mean to me. *Hmm.*

Thankfully, my decision is made for me when he suddenly perks up. He watches something across the street with interest, standing up straight and tall, his short, onyx-black hair getting ruffled in the breeze. After a moment he walks quickly across the street in that stiff way of his that always makes him look like he's in a hurry.

I scurry up to where he was standing and look over to where he was watching before. *Oh! There's a new pie shop? Nice!* We haven't had any kind of bakery here since I was a kid and Old Lady Jensen retired. That is a way healthier option than gas station candy. Pie has some fruit at least, I'm sure.

I make my way across the street and open the door, which has been painted a bubblegum pink color. *Cute.* There is a counter ahead of me where you can see a bunch of pies and other treats on display that can be ordered to-go and an area to wait to be seated to my right. I see Cliff standing near the sign for those who would like to have a table and decide I would like a table, too.

I'm looking at all the adorable vintage pie shop decorations on the walls as I walk toward the seating area. Smiling, all-American pin-up girls holding slices of apple pie salute proudly from over the counter. More mischievous-look-ing girls hang on the wall near the payphone, next to the silky slices of rum raisin on display. The fact that she even has a payphone here is vintage kitsch these days. I'm loving peering at all the wonderful things as I walk further in, so I don't notice the little bump in the rug when I reach it. Of course, being the klutz that I am, I trip over it.

And, because things always have to go doubly wrong, I crash right into Cliff.

"Oof!" My head slams sideways into his chest, a button on his burgundy wool cardigan scraping my cheek as I knock him backward.

"Fucking hell," Cliff barks out as we hit the ground.

We're lying on the ground, me on top of Cliff, when the most beautiful legs I've ever seen step next to me. I turn my face up, delighting in every inch of bare skin I see as I do until the edge of a pair of pink shorts appears. Above the shorts, there is a pink apron and then a white blouse. And above that a downturned face with a very pink frown.

"Get the hell off of me, Trig." Cliff shoves me and my mind returns to the situation at hand.

Rolling off of the other man, I make my way to my feet. Cliff is up quickly, brushing himself off and inspecting for dust or dirt or who knows what. The woman is still standing there in her sweet little outfit, holding a pad of paper and a pencil. Her mouth is turned down into a frown, yes, but her sapphire-blue eyes sparkle with mirth.

"You know there's no need to fight for a table, right? I've got plenty of space." She gestures with one hand tipped in ruby-red nails to the empty dining room. "I haven't even officially announced the opening. You're my first customers."

"Sorry, ma'am. I just tripped on the rug. Kind of a klutz." I nervously scratch the back of my neck as I turn to Cliff. "Sorry to you, too. Didn't mean to knock you down."

"No harm done," he mumbles, looking in the direction of the dining room, which happens to not be in the same direction as my face.

"Oh shoot, it's my fault if it was the rug," interjects the woman as she smooths out the bump. "Why don't each of you pick a table and I'll bring you whatever you want for free as my apology. Is that alright?"

"That would be great!" I grin.

"Thank you, that's very kind," says Cliff before he heads to the table near the front window, farthest from the door. It's the same general position he takes at the café across the street; the same position he's taken every time he's gone there since he was a kid.

We've both lived in this town our whole lives. Since the town is very, very small we can't help but know each other and just about everything there is to know *about* each other. If I know his favorite seating position it's not a surprise, it's just a fact of life. Another fun fact: he can't stand me. Since I've already upset him once today, I won't do it again by sitting too close. I take a table far away from him and wait for the waitress.

Chapter Three
Crystal

Well, shoot. I didn't plan on my first two customers winding up in a tangled heap on the floor. What a gosh darn mess. Hopefully, this isn't a bad omen. I really, really don't need any more bad luck. I put everything I have into this place so everything has to go just right.

I fill up their glasses with ice and water and set them on a tray. Next, I pat my apron pocket to make sure my pad and pencil are in there. *All there.* Putting two paper-wrapped straws and two menus on my tray, I take a deep breath. *Here we go.*

With a big ol' smile on my face, I head out from behind the glass counter. My ponytail bounces behind me and my hips sway side to side in my short, pink shorts. I make my way to the grumpier of the two men first. It's always better to get the grumpy ones taken care of sooner rather than later.

"Your water, sir," I tell him as I set the cold drink and straw down on the bright pink table. "My name's Crystal. Here's your menu."

"I don't need a menu." He sits very straight, his whole body very much wooden in posture. "I would like a slice of traditional apple pie and a cup of black coffee. I'm assuming you have that, of course."

"Oh, sure! What good would a pie shop be without apple pie and coffee?" I take the menu back and set it on my tray. "I'll have that up shortly, hon."

"Thank you, Crystal," he says primly. Though it's not by any means meant to be, the way he says my name sounds pretty darn sexy. I can't place why, it's just something about him that makes me want to scurry to do what he says. *Yum.*

I bounce on my new white sneakers over to the next man to take his order. He still looks quite rumpled from the fall, though I have to wonder if maybe he doesn't always look a little messy. He kind of has that "tornado of a human" feeling about him. I set down his water, straw, and menu.

"Hi there! I'm Crystal. Here's your water and your menu. Why don't you take a minute to decide what you'd like, and I'll be right back."

"Actually, I'm in a bit of a hurry so why don't you just bring me whatever you think is best that's also fast. I teach high school, and the kids always end up throwing things at each other if I'm late. Every single time. Usually food. So messy." He fusses with the edges of his shirt sleeves as he grimaces at the thought of the apparent food fights that take place in his absence.

"Alright then, as long as you don't have any allergies, I'll bring you something special." I laugh. "Be right back."

Well, that one was pretty darn cute, too. If the men in this town are all this good-looking, I'm in serious trouble. Shoot, it only takes one to make trouble. I know that all too well.

Sighing at that thought, I set down my tray on the back counter and wash my hands before getting to work slicing up some pie. I get the apple for the grumpy one and decide on some strawberry rhubarb for the rumpled one. The rhubarb will be a bit fun because he could either love it or hate it, there's rarely an in-between reaction with people and I'd like to see his. I pour some coffee and set it all on my tray, then I adjust my apron, wash my hands again, and head back out.

"Apple pie and black coffee for you." I set the dishes in front of the first man as he sits ramrod straight, hands flat on the edge of the table in front of him. "Is there anything else I can get for you?"

"That will be all." He nods dismissively. I feel a blush come to my cheeks.

"Yes, sir. Let me know if ya need anything," I say with a smile as I walk away with an unnecessary sway to my hips. *Anything is right.*

The man on the other side is fussing with something on his phone when I walk up, and he doesn't notice me at first. I softly clear my throat to get his attention. He startles, dropping his phone and knocking his water over. The water spills over the edge of the table onto the black and white checkered floor.

"Oh gosh, I'm so sorry," he says in a panic as he picks up the cup, getting the cuffs of his shirt wet in the process. "I was looking up something about the Poincaré Conjecture and then I somehow ended up on the Wikipedia page of Pierre-Simon Laplace and I...am going to continue babbling if I don't stop now. If you hand me a mop, I can clean this up."

"I'll get it, don't worry. This pie needs to be eaten and you're the man to do it. Any ol' person can do the mopping. Why don't ya scoot to the next table over, one that doesn't have a flood under it, alright sweetie?" I wink at him to make him feel a little more comfortable and I can see his tense shoulders visibly relax.

"Okay, sounds good. What did you pick for me?" he asks as he moves over to the next table.

"Strawberry rhubarb." I wait for his reaction as I set it down.

He cocks his head as he sits down in the pink vinyl chair, the ones I upholstered myself to match the tables perfectly. Took forever, too.

"I've never had rhubarb. I like trying new things though, so this'll be fun." The smile he tosses me is authentic and I'm relieved to see it.

"It's not for everyone, so if you don't like it, I'll get you something else. But I think if you do like it, it'll be worth the experimenting."

"I love experimenting."

The look he gives me tells me he's not just talking about food. My face goes red hot and, much to my embarrassment, a giggle bubbles out of me. I shake the silliness out of my head and hold my tray nice and high.

"Good to know. If you need anything else give me a holler," my voice a little breathier than intended as I walk away.

Chapter Four
Cliff

Trig. It's always *Trig*. Ever since we were children, he's been a pain in my ass. So of course, when I meet the most beautiful woman I've ever seen, he's there to make a fool out of me.

By the time I finish my pie, the restaurant has begun to fill with curious patrons and I'm unable to speak with the owner, Crystal, for more than the moment it takes to pay my bill. I leave the shop and head north toward the museum, intent on working on the new Benitoite display.

"Hey! Cliff! Hold up!" a familiar voice calls from close behind me.

I increase my pace. *Trig*. Why can't he leave me alone?

"Cliff! Just one sec, I promise." Trig jogs next to me.

My eyebrows scrunch inward, and my jaw clenches, as I lock my gaze forward and increase my pace further. Trig continues to jog next to me, his sandy brown hair flopping into his eyes. He blows the strands out of the way and shakes his head, leaving a tangled mop on top.

"I just want to say sorry is all. That was super embarrassing for you, probably, since you don't like disturbances and stuff. So, I just wanted to, I don't know, apologize. Okay?"

His pale cheeks turn pink as he waits for my response. I only sigh heavily as we approach the museum doors. The apology is genuine. We've known each other long enough to understand more than a little about our reactions and intent. He never means to do anything wrong, but he always does, nonetheless. It's impossible to *hate* him for it because there is no malintent behind his misdeeds, and yet I can't simply overlook all the trouble he causes. If I want to succeed in life, I can't let his mistakes constantly hold me back.

"Have a nice day, Trig," is the best I can do as I walk into the museum, leaving him outside.

It's not quite forgiveness, but it's not admonishment either. It will do.

When I get to my office, I sit at my desk for a moment to make sure everything is where I left it and in the correct place. I need everything lined up exactly the same way every day or I don't feel...right. It's not possible to explain the feeling to most people so I don't bother trying to. They don't need to know why—they only need to know that when things are right, I do my job, and I do it well. When they see my work, they agree, and give me space to do what I need to. If I happen to have exactly three of every item lined up perfectly straight on my desk it doesn't matter to them as long as my department does better than any other museum's geology department in the country. Which it does.

Once I'm sure everything is where it needs to be, I lean back in my seat and take a moment to arrange my thoughts so that I won't be distracted when I get on the department floor. My thoughts of Trig get set away easily; I've had enough practice with him over the years. It takes me longer to deal with the stressful feeling of missing the café today, but that is soothed easier than it would have been due to the pie shop being there. *The pie shop.* My thoughts turn to Crystal.

Yes, she is quite beautiful, but there is something more there. Though I'm rationally aware that her calling me "sir" was simply politeness, I can't help but imagine her using the word in alternate situations. She follows directions beautifully. How I'd love to see how far she'd let me guide her.

My mind wants to wander into dangerous territory, but I shut down every attempt. I need a clear mind for work. When the thoughts have finally settled and I am sure I can focus, I check the clock and see I am exactly on time to return from break. Excellent.

Perhaps tomorrow I might take some pie home after my trip to the café.

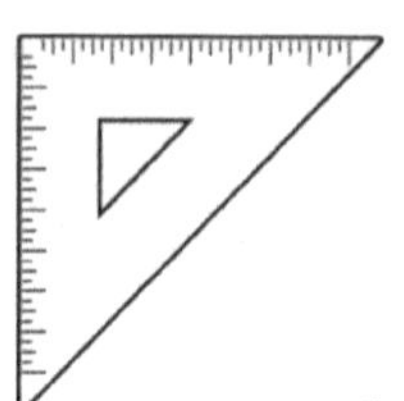

Chapter Five
Trig

A*rgh!* Cliff is so stubborn. I think he forgives me though. Maybe. At least he said something instead of ignoring me. That's more than he does some of the time anyway.

Okay, now I've got to hurry my butt back to the school. It's way on the south end of Main and I'm going to have to dodge the afternoon shoppers as I go. Pausing, I make sure my shoelace is tied before starting; I've learned my lesson after a few too many accidents.

As I jog, my mind wanders to Crystal. She's so pretty. I've never seen hair and eyes combined like that on someone in person before. And that *ass*. Not trying to be crude but, WOW. I wonder if I can just skip the pie next time and have her sit on my face instead. I might suffocate, but it would be worth it.

Ah, dang, I'm getting turned on. That's not good. Running through the busy sidewalk with an erection is likely frowned upon so I better stop this train of thought.

Slowing down, I try to think of something that isn't sexy. Um, uh, Cliff. He was mad. So mad. That made me feel sad.

Oh, and when he gets mad his dark eyes get that fire in them, and he breathes all heavy, and he looks like he wants to wrap his hand around my neck, and...this is actually not helping. Oh my God.

Did I have horny feelings for Cliff? On the sidewalk next to an old man who's wearing a t-shirt that says, "Sexiest Banjo Player 2017"? I'll need to analyze that later. Right now, I'll focus on Sexy Banjo and his sweat stains.

Yep, that worked. By the time I get to the school, I'm back to appropriate teacher mode. I'm five minutes late, but when am I not?

"Hi, kids!" I say as I put my things in the drawer. "Who's ready to learn some geometry today?"

Two of the kids raise their hands, and that makes me smile because that's two more than yesterday. Maybe I'm making a difference here!

Life is good.

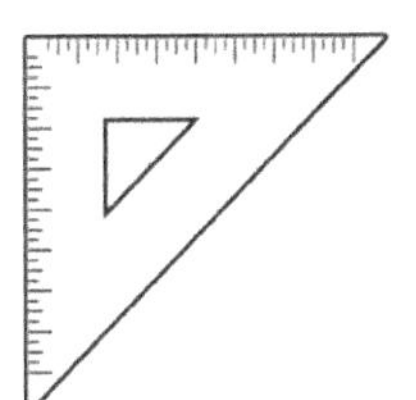

Chapter Six

Crystal

My first day in business was actually really great. Most food was sold out by the end of the day and people seemed to really like what they ate. I've got such a good feeling about the future of the business. If only things outside of work could be so good. *Sigh.*

It's a long drive home from the shop. I can't live in town, as my condition requires me to own a fair amount of private land. Even though it's barely past sundown, I'm pretty tired when I finally turn off the freeway and start up the long driveway to my place.

I park in front of my little, white house, and open the door. A massive creature jumps on me as soon as I unlock it, nearly knocking me back with its huge paws.

"Plato!" I laugh as my Great Dane licks my face. "Get down buddy. Let me put my things away then I'll let you outside, alright? One sec."

Plato sets his paws back on the floor and trots next to me as I put my things down. We walk out the back door and he goes out to relieve himself while I go inside and take a shower. He's such a good dog. I feel bad that he has to be locked up all day. At night, though, he's free range and he's so good about it. Most people wouldn't understand letting a dog roam around all night, but most people don't have Plato. And they don't have the needs I do.

After I get out of the shower, I get Plato back in and give him some food before making myself a dinner of salad out of a bag and reheated pizza. Real exciting, I know. Settling in on the couch, I watch some videos on the internet to keep myself company while I eat. I can't have real company at night, and that kind of life gets mighty lonely. The least I can do is listen to some pretty goth lady review makeup so I can have another person's voice at the table.

After dinner, I lay in bed for a while and read a romance book about big, pink aliens with electrified dicks. I can't have real romance, so may as well go all out in the fantasy.

When I'm done, I make sure I have clean clothes set out for tomorrow, brush my teeth, and sigh once more.

Here it goes again.

"Come on, Plato. It's close to midnight. Time to go."

Locking up the house, I head out into the woods behind it with Plato at my side, my steps heavy with reluctance. I know I have to do this every night, but it never gets better. It always makes me angry. It always hurts.

When I get to the little clearing that I've set up for this task, I strip out of my clothes and put them and my keys into a waterproof bag, then put that bag into a hidden safe. I give Plato a scratch on his head.

"Go on and play. And remember, no bad guys come close to me, alright?"

He gives my cheek a lick before running into the woods, probably going to find some little animal to chase, though he never catches them from what I've seen. I place my hands to my sides and look up to the sky, waiting for midnight.

I know when midnight comes because I feel when the change happens, though I only feel it for a second before everything goes dark. I won't feel, see, or hear anything again until sunrise.

If I were someone able to experience things, however, and I was on the outside looking at me, I would see a strange occurrence happen at midnight.

I would see a woman change in a flash from a human into a pyramid.

A nearly transparent pyramid, as tall as the woman was, three-sided all the way around. The pyramid would stay there, exactly the same until sunrise, when the woman would return in its place, looking the same as she did before.

As angry and hurt as she was before.

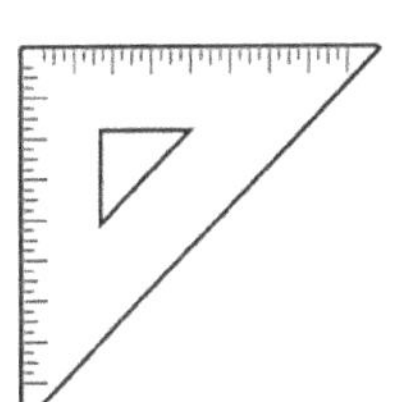

Chapter Seven
Cliff

I'm not ready to give up my lunch at the café. I've been going too long and the thought of changing such a large part of my daily routine fills me with such anxiety it's overwhelming. But I *can* change the part of it that comes after. The variation *is* part of the routine.

Normally I take a short walk, perhaps read a book, or do a crossword puzzle—anything I'm in the mood for. Nothing is set in stone. So, it's perfectly alright if I choose to go to the pie shop and sit for a cup of coffee today.

What's not alright is finding that every table is full when I get there. I *can* take a long break. As long as my work is taken care of it doesn't really matter when it's done. But I prefer to be home at exactly five thirty each day, and if my break is too long, I may not make it. Waiting for a seat is probably not an option. I sigh as I shove my hands into the pockets of my gray cardigan and ready myself to turn back.

That is until I see her walking toward me. She's coming around the counter, that blonde ponytail swinging back and forth in time with her hips. It's at that moment that something inside me growls out an oath to one day have that ponytail wrapped around my fist.

"Well, hi there! My very first customer has come back to me. That's got to be a good sign, right?"

Her smile is magnificent, the light reflecting off her glossy lips, the corners of her sapphire-blue eyes crinkled up with her happiness. That happiness feels so contagious, so pure. How am I going to tell her I have to leave?

"Ah, I see you're quite full, unfortunately. I do have to be home on time so can't wait too long. I must be going."

Her smile falls, and I wonder for a moment if I might not be able to get home a little late after all. My stomach turns thinking about it after already having such a disturbed schedule yesterday. If only someone would leave right now.

"Cliff! Hey Cliff! Come sit with me!" I hear shouted over the chatter in the dining area.

I groan internally when I recognize the voice. *Trig*. Crystal's eyes, however, light up.

"Well, there's your solution! You can sit with your pal!" She waves me in his direction as she begins to walk toward his table.

Fuck. When I watch her perfect ass sashay away, I have no choice but to follow. She sits me across from him, then pulls the pad and pencil from her apron as he smiles boyishly at me. *Annoying*.

"What can I get for you?"

"Just black coffee. I'll be quick today."

"Right away!"

As she goes off to get the coffee, I frown at Trig. His smile falters a bit as he clears his throat.

"How's it going, Cliff? Anything new on the geology front?" he asks awkwardly, scratching the back of his neck the way he does when he's nervous.

"I'm currently working on setting up displays of gems and minerals, which can be anywhere from thousands to billions of years old. So no, nothing new." I watch him, unsmiling, waiting for my coffee so I may drink it and leave.

"Oh, okay." We're quiet for a moment, his head down, before he looks up again, directly into my eyes. "Cliff, I'm really sorry about when we were young. I know you're still mad, but it really was an accident."

"That's enough," I cut him off. "I'm not getting into this with you again. Especially not here."

At that moment, Crystal returns with the coffee. She sets it down in front of me and pours just the right amount into the cup without me having to tell her when to stop.

"Anything else for you two?"

Your telephone number.

"That will be all, thank you," I say.

"That's it for me!" echoes Trig.

"Well then, here are your checks. Come to the register when you're ready to pay."

She walks away and it feels like I can't drink my coffee fast enough, even though it practically scalds my throat. Not only to get away from Trig but to see her again, if only for the moment it takes to pay my bill.

"Cliff, can we please be friends again some-day? We were so good together."

Trig stops me cold with that question. An apology I expected—he's made many of those over the years. Outright asking to be friends again is another thing entirely.

"You know how difficult change is for me, Trig. I spent every single day with you. You were almost my entire routine. And yet, I dropped you easily. No, we will never be friends again. Goodbye, Trig."

I stand up then and pay my bill. Seeing Crystal doesn't feel as good as I thought it would. Not because she isn't amazing—she very much is. The problem is I'm too busy choking to focus on her.

Lies are difficult to swallow.

Chapter Eight
Trig

"You alright, sugar?"

Crystal struts up to my table and pauses, one hand on her hip. She looks down at me with genuine concern and my heart warms. At least someone in this town gives a damn.

"I'm okay. Just an old wound opening up is all. It'll be fine." I offer her a smile that I know doesn't really reach my eyes, but I try anyway.

"If you want to talk about it, I close at five. Give me an hour to close shop, then you can come back for a cup of coffee and a chat to get things off your chest. Seems like you could use it."

My brain short circuits for a second, and I don't answer. I can't tell if she's asking me to meet her in a romantic context, a friendly context, or if she thinks I'm pathetic and she's trying to take pity on me. I mean, I guess I'll say yeah either way. If it's not romantic I can try to convince her with my manly charms to want me.

"Hon? You there? You're awful quiet." Her brow pinches in concern as she inspects my silent face. The face that's been silent for a good twenty seconds since she asked her question.

"Oh, uh, sorry. I spaced out. Yes, I would like to meet up. At six. Here. Coffee." *You sound like a moron, Trig, good job.* Very manly and charming.

"Sounds good then. Your lunch is on me today. See ya later." She winks as she swishes away to speak with another table.

I get up and immediately leave; it's time to get back to the school and finish as much of my work as possible so that I can get home quickly and take my time getting ready for this date. Well, not date. Friendly meeting. I think. I don't know. Either way, I should at least brush my teeth, do something about my hair, and put on a clean shirt.

When I get back to the school, I discover that I am very behind in grading papers. This is not unusual. Luckily, when I get in the zone and really focus on something, which is unfortunately difficult, I can accomplish things quickly and efficiently. Maybe I ignore the children a little bit but it's not like they care. I tell them to create their best math inspired dance for social media and they go for it with gusto.

By the end of the day, I'm caught up on everything and the kids actually enjoyed math. Maybe I need to date more often. Not date, friendly meeting. Whatever.

I head home on my bicycle. I could drive, I do have a car, but I'm so close to the school it would be silly. Plus, I just think it's nice not to clog up the air with poison if I don't have to. And it's good exercise too. Yeah, bicycles are great.

When I get home, I lock my bike up on the porch and happily skip through my red front door. My house is small but comfortable. And messy. Not dirty, just cluttered. I've never been particularly good at organization, and I'm very sentimental, so throwing things out is tough. I don't mean garbage, just stuff.

For example, there's a pile of clean laundry on my sofa that I've needed to fold for...well, I don't think I've ever folded it. I just kind of find what I want to wear and take it. And I have a habit of buying more books than I have shelf space for so there are a lot of them, uh, everywhere. It's that kind of stuff that makes my house a mess.

Someday, if someone decides I'm good enough to raise a family with, I'll need to take care of it. But for now, it's just my mess to live with.

And my cat, Pytha. She's the best cat. I pour some food into the bowl for the tabby and re-place her water with fresh stuff. She rubs her-self around my legs before beginning to chomp away happily at her food. She's so cute.

Checking the time, I see that I've got a good bit before I need to meet Crystal, so I decide to hop in the shower. I make sure I actually bring the new bottle of body wash *into* the shower with me this time and don't forget it on the counter still in the shopping bag like I did this morning. I tend to forget a lot of little things like that.

I definitely cannot forget how great Crys-tal looked today though. As I'm scrubbing up, I think of her perky chest, thick thighs, and pleasantly plump backside. I stroke myself absently at first, daydreaming of her smile and her tiny shorts. When I start thinking of what's under those shorts, I grip my cock tighter and begin jacking off in earnest.

I wonder if she's smooth between her thighs or if she has that icy blonde hair over her sweet cunt. What the nipples on her small breasts look like. My breath comes out in harsh pants as I think about sinking between those thick thighs, about the sounds she'd make. I think about her crying out my name.

"Trig, yes, fuck me," she'd cry out. "I want your cock. You and Cliff. Both of you, now."

I gasp in confusion and desire as Cliff enters my thoughts, crouching behind Crystal, his hand gently holding her throat, his eyes locked on mine.

"I'm here, Crystal. I'm going to fuck your sweet ass," he purrs against her ear. I pump my cock into my fist fast, my movements frantic. "Then when you've had enough, I'll finish inside Trig."

I explode onto the shower floor in the hardest orgasm I've had in years. It feels like nev-

er-ending ropes of cum stream out of me before I'm spent. When I'm done, I stand there,
water spraying onto me, a bewildered expression on my face.

What the fuck was that?

Chapter Nine
Crystal

Oh boy. Why did I ask that man to come over? This is nothing but trouble. He just looked so damn pathetic. And handsome. So very, very handsome.

Ugh. What's wrong with me? You'd think I learned my lesson with Chad. *Don't be a fool for a handsome face.* Ah well, I'll just have to make sure he doesn't stay long and then I'll drive home quick. No serious crushes allowed.

When the doors are locked and everything is wiped clean, I hear a tap on the front window. A pleasantly pale face with wind-blushed cheeks smiles at me through the glass. Gosh, he looks so young sometimes; this flash makes him look like he's maybe starting college at best. His eyes are so bright, his skin clear, his hair thick, lips full and rosy. He would look perfect in one of those advertisements at that clothing store that was popular in the early 2000s. You know, the one that hired only hot, preppy-type people? And they had shirtless men on the shopping bags? He has a perfect face for that sort of thing. But the rest of him is just chaos.

I open the door and the end of his scarf flaps in the wind, slapping him in the face. Trig pulls it off, spitting out bits of wool fuzz. He pulls off his stocking cap as he steps inside, and his hair sticks up in a staticky halo.

"Hi, Crystal! It's chilly out there this evening. Hope you brought a jacket!" He smiles, and for the first time, I notice he has one slightly crooked tooth among his otherwise straight, white teeth. Somehow that makes him even more adorable.

"Oh yep, I brought one. I always check the weather forecast before I go out. I've lived a lot of places, so I know how to adjust to different climates."

"Oh, you've moved around a lot? How come?" he asks as he takes a seat at the table nearest to the door.

I shuffle my feet nervously for a moment before taking the seat across from him. I'm going to avoid questions about me as long as I can. Don't really want to explain the whole being a freak thing right now.

"It's complicated. Plus, we're here for you, not me. I want you to tell me what's going on so you can stop being a Gloomy Gus in my restaurant." *Nice save.*

He lowers his eyes as he wrings his hands, silent for a moment. His face looks older now, no longer that boy.

"It's just Cliff and I, we have a history. He hates me. There's nothing I can do to fix it. When he decides something is one way then it's that way forever. He's decided he can't stand me and that's that. It sucks."

"Did you do something truly unforgivable? Why is he so angry?" I cock my head to the side wondering what could have caused such a rift between them. Trig seems like a genuinely sweet guy, and I can't imagine him doing anything malicious to Cliff, or anyone.

"To him I did. But it was an accident. I never meant to hurt him. He was my best friend. I would have done anything for him. I thought he felt the same, but then one day he just dropped me and never took me back."

We're quiet while Trig closes his eyes, taking a few deep breaths. When he's calm and his eyes are open again, I continue to speak.

"Will you tell me what happened? Maybe you need to talk about it." Plus, I admit I'm a curious cat, but that's beside the point.

"Sure, I guess. It's a little long but I'll do it."

"Okay," I say with a nod. "Bring it on."

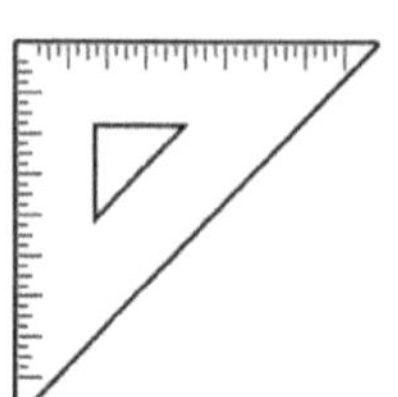

Chapter Ten

Trig

T en years ago, Cliff and I shared a room in college. I was finishing my degree in mathematics, and he was working on his in geology. We were both at the top of the class and feeling good about our futures.

I knew I was eventually going to move back to Isawsa Falls. This place needed a good math teacher, and I wanted to be it. Cliff, on the other hand, wanted out. He knew his limits and what he wanted to do. His life here had been awful, frankly, and having to come home was his nightmare. He knew ideally, he wanted to work for a museum, and he wanted to work for a prestigious one.

I was sad to see him go, as I told him many times, but we agreed to meet wherever he went. Because we were best friends. Really. We never spent more than a day or two apart since we *were little kids. I knew everything about him, and I knew why he wanted out.*

Cliff hated Isawsa Falls because his parents were here. His parents were terrible people. They never understood that Cliff is just a little different from most people. His brain operates differently, and traditional ways of doing things won't always work for him. When he couldn't fit their mold, they were very...well, they were not good to young Cliff. He escaped to my house as often as he could where he could line things up the way he liked, eat the things he liked, move and speak in the ways that were comfortable for him. And I liked it. I liked him and just being near him. And he accepted my differences, even if they drove him nuts sometimes.

Like, when we were little, he spent hours making a perfectly symmetrical sandcastle and lined up all the seashells he found by smallest to largest around it. It was really cool. But I got distracted by an awesome eagle flying overhead. When I went running over excitedly to show him, I looked up too far, fell backward, and crushed his castle. But he forgave me because we still went to the beach together and played instead of him being stuck with his mom and dad.

And he hated how messy my room was. But I would just get so overwhelmed by tasks, back before I learned coping mechanisms. A stack of laundry was like Mount Everest to me. He would come over and have to clean up with a frustrated look on his face every time before he felt comfortable in my room, and I felt bad, but I was grateful he did it. And I didn't want to wait hours to clean it before telling him he could come over, anyway.

The point is, he knew I was a mess, and I knew he liked things just so. Yet we worked out as friends because we just liked each other as people. I always defended him and took care of him when no one else would. He always picked me up when I fell and we accepted each other's faults. I thought what we had would outlast anything.

Well, Cliff had a chance to work in the geology department of the most prestigious museum in the country. It was his real chance to escape from this place and live the life he'd planned for himself. Gosh, I was so proud of him and so excited for him.

He had to download a special program for the museum's security to even apply for the position, so he did and was working on the application. It was nearly done but needed a few more tweaks, according to him. He was almost guaranteed the position as long as he got the application in by the end of that week.

But then, yeah, I screwed everything up.

He told me not to touch the computer (it was our shared computer; neither of us were well off) while he was out visiting with a mutual friend. I didn't plan on it, but then I heard there was a limited time event in an online game I liked to play.

I don't know why I decided to play it instead of listening to Cliff. It was just some dumb spur-of-the-moment decision. Back then I was a lot worse about making thoughtless choices, I guess. Anyway, I booted up the game and started to play.

I don't know how, but somehow the program that had Cliff's application opened as well. The keys I was pressing to move and shoot in the game started appearing as their corresponding letters in the text boxes of the application. Instead of a perfectly worded form, it was now filled with many combinations of mostly W,A,S,D, and Q. And that was before it hit send.

I got off the game before Cliff came home and barely noticed that the other program was open. I just closed it without thinking anything of it. The next day, Cliff spent the morning at school and when he came home in the late afternoon, he checked his personal emails. In that inbox he found one rejection letter from a prestigious museum telling him he wasn't funny and to not bother them again.

Cliff was panicking like I'd never seen him. He walked in circles, pulling at his hair. He even flapped his hands in this upset way like he hadn't since we were little, making this terrible almost screeching noise. All the time asking "What the fuck? What happened? I don't understand!"

I didn't understand at first either. Until I pulled up the sent files and looked at the image. Then I remembered closing out the app after I closed my game. I put two and two together and...yeah.

He stared at me for a long time after I told him. He was stone still and so quiet I couldn't even tell *if he was breathing or not. But he did speak after a while.*

"I want you to leave. I am asking you to move out."

My eyebrows flew up. "What? Why?"

"Why?" He scoffed. "You just ruined my dreams, Trig. My chance to get away, to make something of myself. All because you couldn't keep your word to me for a few measly hours. I'm tired of cleaning up your messes. I've been doing it for so long. You wreck everything, and I'm especially done when this is a mess that can't be fixed."

I was so shocked, I just nodded my head and started packing. Even with my executive dysfunction issues, I managed to pack everything because I was so zoned out thinking about what the hell was going on. I knew I fucked up, and really badly, but he'd never been like that before.

When I finished packing, he didn't even say goodbye as I left. He just watched me go, hands stiff at his sides, the way he'd watch a stranger. I ended up going to stay with another friend for the rest of the semester before moving back home.

I moved back to Isawsa Falls and eventually got a teaching position. I was glad about it, but I missed Cliff. His parents both died in an accident; I don't think they were missed by many. I tried to reach out to him, but he never responded.

Then I saw him on Main Street one day and heard him say to the tailor he was moving back. I was so happy. But that was soon crushed when I tried to talk to him.

"Get away from me. Nothing has changed. You stay on your side of the highway; I'll stay on mine." He stiffly walked away toward the museum, leaving me alone in the street with an ache in my stomach and tears in my eyes. And nothing has changed between us since.

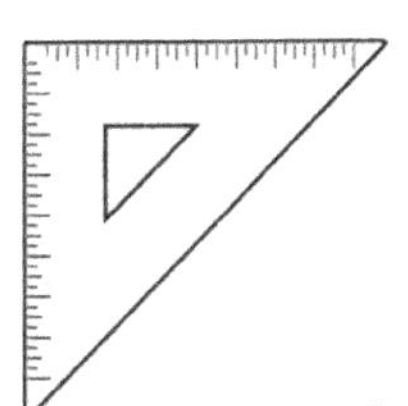

Chapter Eleven
Crystal

"**O**h, you poor thing. That's not fair at all. You made a mistake. He shouldn't punish you so harshly."

Though I have to admit to myself that it sounds like Trig really was a mess back then.

Trig sighs and slumps in his seat. "There's just no getting through to him."

"It's his loss then. You're a real sweetheart, I can just tell," I say with a smile.

I'm not trying to flirt so I make sure my voice is bright, cheery, and nowhere near seductive. I can't afford to flirt and risk bringing trouble to this town. He is so gosh darn cute though.

I do allow myself to place my hand on top of Trig's in a gesture of comfort. His smooth skin is warm and pleasant, and though his fingers are delicate, they're still strong when they turn and interlace with mine. Trig closes his eyes and relaxes while I comfort him.

It's good that his eyes are closed because then something real weird happens, and I don't want him to see it.

Where he holds my hand, it glows a bright greenish-blue and is kind of see-through. My eyes widen and my jaw drops at the sight of it. *What the hell?*

I take my hand out of his and slap it into my lap under my other hand to hide it. He opens his eyes, brow furrowed in confusion, eyes turned down in what appears to be sadness.

"I'm sorry, it's just that you scratched me," is all that I can think to say.

It's not entirely a lie because it *might* be an injury—I don't know yet. Either way, the excuse seems to work because the look of sadness and confusion clears up into understanding. He nods.

"Ah, sorry. I'm very accident-prone. I hope you aren't too hurt?"

"No, it's fine, I was just surprised."

"Okay good. Because if you need me to get you anything, I can." He sits up at attention, ready to help.

"No, really, it's fine. Are you okay? Like, emotionally?" Time to turn this back to the topic at hand and then get him out of here quick.

"I'm feeling much better just having been able to talk about it, actually. I know he doesn't want to fix things but being reminded that I was just an idiot, and not someone who was cruel or something, is helpful. So, thanks."

I genuinely smile at that. I'm so happy to help this man. I glance down at my hands and see they're no longer glowing. Alright, this is a good time for him to go.

"Trig, hon, I have to get going. Sorry to kick you out so fast. My dog is gonna need me."

"Oh! I love dogs! Go take care of him and give him a snuggle for me!" Trig grins as he buttons his coat back up. "And if you're cold or lonely you can maybe give yourself a snuggle from me too."

His cheeks turn bright red, and he looks away from me as he tugs on his hat. I can't help but let out a girlish giggle that I should be embarrassed by at my age, but it makes him break out in a crooked grin back at me.

"Oh, you," I say as I walk him to the door. "I'm sure Plato will appreciate the hug."

Maybe he'll get the point that I'm only considering the dog part of his offer. Whatever point he gets however just makes his grin broader as he steps past the threshold.

"Goodnight, Crystal."

"Goodnight, Trig."

He brushes a hand against mine as he leaves before turning and walking away. As I reach up to lock the door, I see where he brushed against me isn't glowing. *Maybe I imagined it before.*

But if I didn't imagine it—and this is what I think it is—I'm about to break my curse. Now where am I supposed to find the other third?

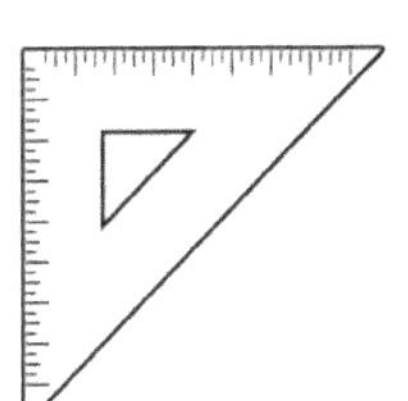

Chapter Twelve
Cliff

Canned soup. Apple sauce. Buttered white bread. An acceptable dinner. Everything looks and tastes the same each time I prepare it. There are no surprise scents or weird textures. I eat it alone and do not have to worry about anything while I do.

People don't understand why I'm so restrictive about things. Sometimes even I don't, I'll admit, but most of the time it seems obvious to me.

I have a set few items of clothing I wear because they are comfortable, fit well, look nice, and I don't have to decide from a million different things when I'm getting dressed.

I prefer to keep three of everything on my desk because I like to always have a backup, and if someone comes in and needs to use one there will be a backup if both fail. It's a legitimate issue; people come to my desk frequently.

I don't understand why people think it's so strange for me to want to be prepared. Keeping them tidy and in the exact same spot each time only helps me to know where everything is and saves me from ever having to dig around for things.

Anyway, the point is, people see me as rigid and difficult and refuse to take the time to understand why I do the things I do. I build up quite a bit of frustration by the end of the day trying to mask my natural inclinations in times when they would make people uncomfortable. So, at night I need to take out those frustrations somehow. Now that I'm done with dinner, I will do that.

I've lived out of the main area of town since I moved back. I knew if I was going to live here, I was going to need space to burn off pent-up energy and this place has a wooded area around it. As my parents died suddenly, and they had no wills and I was their next of kin, I received their small inheritance. It was enough for the down payment here. My closest neighbor is a quarter mile away and I haven't even met them. They only moved in recently since Mr. Jones passed away. I have a lot of room to roam and I'm going to use as much of it as I can tonight.

My closet holds only a few garments. Three pairs of pants, three sweaters, and three shirts. In a drawer, I have six undershirts, six pairs of socks, and six pairs of underwear. I have one suit and tie in a dry-cleaning bag. I have one pair of boots, one pair of sneakers, and three identical pairs of my favorite shoes, two in black and one in brown. I have two pairs of pajamas. These are my normal clothes, and they are all organized exactly the way I like them.

I do, however, have a few more things hidden in two satchels at the bottom of the closet. One is for...different activities I need not think of now. In another, however, there is a t-shirt, a hooded sweatshirt, and a pair of running pants. There is a second pair of sneakers that is not as well-kept as my daily option in a plastic bag. These are the clothes I will wear tonight.

I feel odd dressed like this, but I know it's necessary for my excursion. I may get dirty, or tangled up, or snagged on something and I don't want to ruin my normal clothes. Plus, I'll be moving quickly so I need to be comfortable. I zip up the sweatshirt and raise the hood. It's chilly tonight, and until I get my blood pumping, I'm sure I'll be cold.

The cold air taunts me as I step out my back door. *Come chase the breeze. You'll never outrun it.* I stretch for a moment before finding the direction of the wind and taking off in a burst of speed.

The wood is dark, and I know running like this with no light is dangerous. That's alright. Whatever happens now is meant to be. I'm following the wind, letting it take me away.

Like it took me to Trig so many years ago. *Fuck.* I almost trip thinking of it. My parents had screamed and screamed at me again because I wouldn't eat mashed potatoes. I just couldn't do it. They didn't understand that it wasn't that I just didn't like them, it was almost as if I was going to be physically ill or in pain every time the white mush came near me. It was torture. But they yelled and accused me of being a spoiled brat. I was so little. I can't understand how someone could be so cruel to such a small child.

When they left the room, I took off out the front door, having no idea where I was going to go, just knowing I needed to leave. I saw the wind blowing leaves one way and decided that way was good enough.

After a bit of running, I saw a boy from my school outside bouncing a ball. I stopped in front of him, too shy to say anything. But Trig always was one to start a conversation.

"Hey, you! I know you! Whatcha cryin' about? You wanna come play?"

I nodded and came forward to catch the ball he threw to me. When I tossed it back, it hit him in the stomach, causing a great 'Oof' to escape the boy's mouth. I cringed but he only laughed.

"Oh boy, you're strong! We gotta play dodgeball together and whoop the other guys. What's your name? You wanna come in for dinner? My mom is making probably soup or something, she's not a good cook is what she says, but I like it okay."

After that, we played nearly every night for years. I wonder if I ran long enough, hard enough, would the wind bring me back to him? If it did, would I stop again for him?

I run harder; old wounds being wrenched wide open in my mind. This was not the plan for tonight but if it's what's needed then so be it. I run through the dark until all of a sudden, it's not quite as dark.

I've got to the clearing, the area that means I've gone too far into the neighbor's land. Normally that's all the clearing is to me, just an empty spot telling me I've run too far. But tonight, it contains a sensational discovery.

In the clearing is a massive tetrahedron, some sort of translucent stone. There is an energy radiating off of it that is indescribable. I feel drawn to it, as if I need to touch it. So, I do.

I run my hand down the smooth triangular side and a ripple of lust runs through me. I gasp and pull my hand away, watching a glow light up everywhere my hand laid upon the stone. A sudden ache in my groin makes me double over. I nearly fall to my knees, but I catch myself with one hand resting on the side of the huge pyramid of crystal.

Touching that stone again causes my cock to go rock hard, my mouth gaping as my breath shudders out of me. A wild need overcomes me, and I can think of nothing else but how beautiful the tetrahedron is.

I look at the way it glows where the heat of my hand lands. I think maybe it's made of fluorite. What a lovely, delicate stone. I groan as I rub my crotch against one of the faces of the stone. *Mmm*, how *smooth* the face of it is. How sharp the *angles*. Oh, *fuck* if this is *fluorite* it might *glow* under a UV light. That would be so beautiful. So, so *beautiful*.

I wrap one arm around the triangular beauty and pull my cock out of my pants with my other hand. As I stroke the rock I stroke my cock, faster and faster, until finally, I splatter the shining crystal with my hot cum.

I step back, putting my cock away, panting. My head finally begins to clear, and I look around me, fully realizing my situation.

I just fucked a rock.

What the fuck?

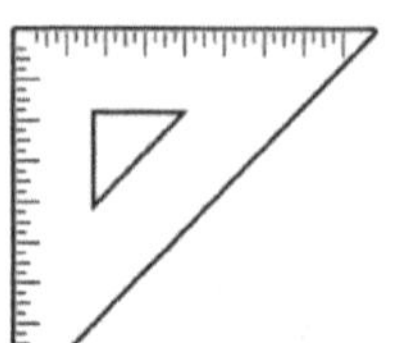

Chapter Thirteen

Crystal

Tonight, when I transform something is different. Tonight, for the first time, not everything goes away while I'm in my pyramid form. This time I can *hear*.

At first, I only hear the normal sounds of the forest, but it's enough to make me pretty darn excited. Don't get me wrong, it's scary as hell to be locked in a form blind, unfeeling, and unable to move, but to be able to experience any type of sense at all is exciting as heck.

After a short while of hearing the normal sounds of wind blowing and little animals rustling through the dead leaves, I hear something different. At first, I think it might be Plato coming around, but then the sound becomes unmistakable: human footsteps.

Oh no. No one is supposed to see me like this. If people discover me like this and start poking around, then I'm going to have to move homes again, and I really don't want to. Shoot, I don't think I can even afford to right now. I haven't made back enough money from the shop yet.

The sound of running footsteps in the leaves slows to a walk, coming closer and closer until it's right next to me. There is a moment of silence and then I hear...that cannot be what I hear.

It's been a while but, um, that sounds like a man *enjoying* himself. Right next to me. What kind of man would see a giant triangular crystal and start jacking off? It makes me think of...wait. Could it be? Is *this* what the curse was talking about? That trashy woman *would* do something like that. *Argh.*

Footsteps leave the clearing, and the forest returns to its normal sounds. I can't help thinking of the past now though, unable to enjoy the sounds around me. That stupid curse. It ruined my life, and I didn't even do anything wrong.

Ten years ago already, that freaking Miranda and I were best friends. I knew she was boy-crazy, but she was always nice to me so long as boys weren't involved. I wasn't particularly interested in dating, more focused on studying business, so it was never a problem.

I also knew Miranda was special. She was the first to reveal to me that there were things in this world beyond that which most people knew. Her family could do some pretty incredible things. She called herself a sorceress and I thought that was pretty darn neat that she trusted me enough to tell me. We really were good friends.

Then she started dating Chad. They started out as a fine couple. She loved him so much, she really did. He seemed to love her too, but it was always clear she loved him just a little more. Well, maybe a lot more.

That divide only grew as time passed, but Miranda didn't see it. She was obsessed with him. It became hard to even be her friend because he was all she wanted to talk about. I still stuck by her though; well, until she started getting paranoid.

One day, she asked if I thought Chad was handsome and I said "I guess" because I didn't know what else to say. He was alright looking, I suppose, but mostly I didn't want to offend her by saying he was only okay. She took that, however, as I wanted to have sex with him or something, and she got really upset. It took a lot of convincing to calm her down.

One day I was staying late after class and who should come in but stupid Chad. He asked me if Miranda was still in love with him, and I said yes. He told me he didn't know how he felt about her anymore and I told him that was his business, not mine. Then he told me he was actually attracted to me.

That's when Miranda showed up. I don't know if she had been there the whole time or if it was terrible timing but either way, she was understandably ticked off at what she heard. It didn't take long for her to start drawing in power from around her for her spell. I tried to stop her, but she was crazy.

"You wanna be a part of a love triangle? How about you be the whole thing?"

She threw some crystals on the ground and said some words I didn't understand. The whole place shook, and I felt sick to my stomach. I couldn't move to stop her; it was like my feet were glued to the floor.

"Because I still care for you like a fool, I'll give you the days until midnight to try and break the curse. But after that, each night until sun-rise you'll take the form of your betrayal. If you can find TWICE as much love as I feel for Chad, you can stop the curse. But even after you're free, you'll still be transparent on the full moon. Transparent as a reminder that I saw through your lies. No betrayals like you betrayed me. Now get the fuck out and never show your face around me again before I change my mind about giving you a chance to break the curse."

I felt my stomach lurch as an invisible force shoved me toward the door. I ran as fast as I could, leaving Chad behind. When I got past the doorway, the door slammed shut. Shortly after that, his screaming began. I didn't stop running until I got home, and I never saw either of them again.

Since then, I've turned into the triangular Crystal every night. It's been over ten years. I've never been able to hear in that form. What's changed?

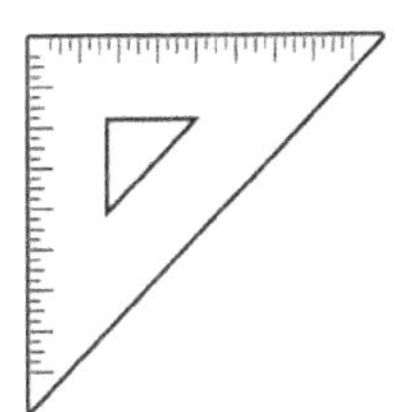

Chapter Fourteen

Trig

Ah, what a wonderful day. The sun is shining brightly, the leaves are green, and a beautiful woman is smiling at me. Nothing could make this day better.

"Well, hello, Trig," Crystal calls out to me as I approach the pie shop. "I saved you a slice of pecan pie."

My favorite. Well, I guess the day could get better after all. It's Friday after school and I'm starting my weekend. Normally, I'd spend the afternoon in the bigger town getting groceries or whatever else I need, or catching up on chores or work, stuff like that. Then, in the evening, I'd maybe get a beer and a burger at the bar in town with the locals. Maybe I can get Crystal to join us tonight.

"Pecan is my favorite. How did you know?" I ask as I jog the last few steps to her.

"I didn't but I guessed. You got that nutty vibe about you," she says with a wink, and I can't help but laugh.

"I've been called a nut more than once so that's fair. Called a lot worse than that, that's for sure. But you can call me anytime." Now it's my time to wink and her time to laugh.

"Wow, that might just have been the corniest pickup line I've ever heard."

"Well, you recognized it as a pickup line, so it didn't fail entirely." I watch as a blush blooms on her round cheeks, and I grin. "Did it fail? Or may I call you sometime?"

With the last question I pause outside the doorway, my voice taking on a serious tone. I know it's a weird time to ask her out but it just kind of came on naturally. Well, I shot my shot. No going back.

"I...things are complicated with me, Trig." Her shoulders slump, and she frowns.

"Are you spoken for, then? I'm sorry, I didn't mean to butt into your relationship."

"No, it's just that I have some weird, um, we'll just say baggage for now."

"Oh. Don't we all?" I take the edge of her apron, futz with the fabric, and wait until she looks into my eyes. "Crystal, if you're not interested in me romantically, you can tell me now and I'll never bother you again, I swear. I'm not one of those creeps who pressure women, okay? But if you're turning me down because you've got some issues, then I think you should reconsider. I can handle a lot and if you have boundaries, I'll respect them. Trust me. I just really like you, and I think you like me too, and it would be a shame if we never got a chance to even try things out, that's all."

Crystal's breath hitches before she lets it out. She shakes her head and fans her face with her hand.

"Alright. One date, okay? We see how it goes. Tomorrow. We'll go for an early afternoon picnic in the woods behind my house. My big, very protective dog will be there, as well as my security cameras and other security measures I'm keeping secret." The stern look she gives me tells me I better nod back seriously without laughing or taking offense, so I do. She gets out her phone and I get out mine. "Here's my number. Text me later and we'll exchange details. My new employee must be going nuts without me right now, so I gotta be getting back inside."

I follow her in, the world's biggest grin on my face. I take a seat and daydream about how our date will go, and don't even notice when Cliff first enters the room.

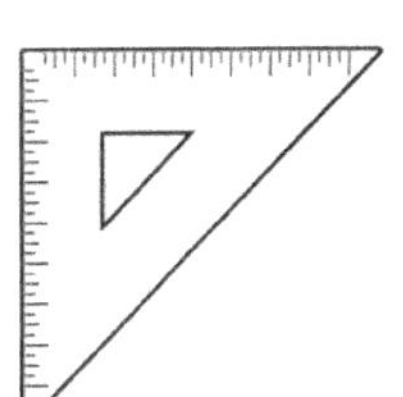

Chapter Fifteen
Cliff

I linger in the shadows, waiting for Crystal to return to the shop. Her employee may well be a fine server, but I must have the same waitress every day and Crystal is that person. It doesn't hurt that I also want to put her over the counter, tug down those little pink shorts, and–

"One date, okay?" I hear her say to *Trig*.

I barely listen to the rest of what they say other than to confirm that yes, they are going out together. *This is madness.* Trig of all people! Yes, he's handsome and kind, but he's *Trig*.

The wind rustles my hair as it blows toward the entrance to the pie shop. My jaw is hanging open in disbelief, but I snap it closed. She promised him *one* date. That means she's free after that. I follow the wind to the door of the shop and enter.

"Well, hi there, Cliff! I kept your regular table free for you and made sure to save a slice of apple just in case," Crystal says with a nod of her head in the direction of said table.

"Thank you, Crystal. I will take that apple pie, indeed." *Fuck*, she's such a good girl.

Smoothing out my wind-blown hair, I follow her to my table. Yes, I've already come to think of it as *my* table, and it seems she's come to as well. Good. I like it when things fit smoothly into place.

"I'll be right back with your coffee and pie, hon." With a swing of her hips, she leaves, and I'm left alone to ponder my next move.

Should I wait to ask her out after she goes out with Trig or ask her out before she goes? If I wait until after she might accept a second date, become attached to him, and I potentially lose my chance. If I ask before she might decline if she's the type of woman to only accept one date at a time. There are many more pros and cons to both options. This is a tough choice. I'll eat my pie and decide.

"Here you go. Enjoy!" Crystal pats me on the shoulder before walking away, and I feel my eyebrows raise. *Touching is a good sign.*

I turn my head slightly to look after her but catch *Trig* in my vision. *Damn.* Thankfully he's watching her with a goofy look of adoration and doesn't notice me. Shoving an uncharacteristically large bite of pie into my mouth, I begin to wolf the slice down. Despite the heat of the coffee, I practically chug it, so it takes me no time at all to finish and sit back in my seat, hands folded neatly in front of me. Crystal steps to my side, handing me my check with raised brows.

"Well, you're mighty hungry today, aren't you? Got some place to be?"

I clear my throat before diving headfirst into my decision. "Crystal, I need to speak with you. Is there a chance we could step to the side briefly?"

"Oh, sure. One sec. Let me meet you over by the entryway, if that's alright?"

"That would be fine." I nod as I stand.

Crystal heads to the counter and I head to the front door. When I get outside, to my relief,

I see no townspeople wandering about this area of the sidewalk who could listen in. Good. For better or worse, I don't want anyone to hear what is about to happen.

"Okay then, hon. What's going on?" Crystal asks as she steps outside, wrapping her arms around herself.

The day is a little chillier than expected. Her nipples perk up under her thin, white blouse and I have to force my stuttering mind back to attention.

"Crystal, would you do me the honor of allowing me to escort you to dinner this weekend?" I clasp my hands behind my back and attempt to look as harmless as possible. Not that I would ever cause anyone harm. Spanking isn't harmful, is it?

"Oh, dear, no." She bites her lip and wrings her hands. "I'm sorry but I can't go out to dinner with you."

My eyelids flutter in disbelief. This is not how I expected this to go, I must admit.

"Alright then. My apologies for bothering you."

"No, no! That's not it! I just can't go out at night. I have a thing, and I can't really talk about it, but it just means dinner is out. My days are free though," she blushes.

I can feel the corners of my lips twitch in the barest hint of a rare smile.

"Days are just fine. Of course, I do work on weekdays."

"Tomorrow morning, I'm busy. What about Sunday, a late breakfast or early lunch?" She bites her lip and all I can think about is biting it for her. "Cliff? Did you hear me?"

"Yes, sorry, I was double checking my schedule. Sunday is fine. Please, let us exchange contact information so that we may make more detailed plans." I take out my phone and she takes a notepad out of the pocket of her apron.

"Sounds good. There's one more thing I should tell you. I think it's kind of important." Her smile has disappeared now and I'm sure I know why.

I nod for her to continue as I write my number on her notepad.

"Oh boy. Well, I'm going on a date tomorrow with another guy. It's a first date too." She shuffles her feet and watches my expression carefully.

"That's fine. I don't expect exclusivity before we've even had one date."

She still doesn't relax, and I know it's because the hardest part is coming.

"Yeah, but the guy is someone you know. It's, well, it's Trig. I know he's your...friend. Is that gonna be weird for you?"

"No." A *lie*. "Though you may need to ask if it will be for him. He may not be as evolved as I am."

I sniff and adjust my collar as she programs her number into my phone. Now if he says anything negative about her dating me, he'll seem like an asshole.

"Oh, that's such a relief. I just can't wait!"

"Neither can I, Crystal."

I follow her back into the shop to pay for my food, then leave. There is somewhere I like to go on Friday nights when everyone else is in town at the bar.

This town has nothing for me but the museum, so when given a choice, I do not spend my time here. On Fridays, I drive to the city to let off the steam I build up during the week that even running can't help. It's when I find people who like to let someone take control. I go to a place where I happen to be very popular, where there is always an abundance of submissive men and women to choose from who'll beg to spend the evening with me. To please me. To let me take *control.* This Friday, I need that release.

After going home and grabbing the other bag I keep in my closet, I change into the clothes I keep inside it, then bring the rest of the items I keep in there to my car. These things aren't items I'd like to have around the house should anyone pop by and take a look around. I'd rather not explain my...hobby, and it's hard to explain away a satchel of handcuffs, whips, and the like as anything other than what I do.

Tonight, as I walk into the Velvet Cuff underground club, I may not be dressed the same as I usually am but that's good. Few from town would recognize me like this, even with such a simple change. I don't normally prefer to draw attention to myself but on these nights, I like to look my best. Running and daily exercise keeps me fit so the tight, black clothes I wear are perfectly tailored to highlight all my best features.

The neckline of my shirt dips just low enough to reveal the tattoos on my chest. Much of my body is covered in tattoos. The folks in the town have no idea, and I prefer it that way. Keeping them a secret is part of why I enjoy having them.

The low lighting of the club reveals a fresh crop of faces along with the familiar ones. A woman in a pink latex mini-dress is perched on the edge of a black, velvet chair in the back corner of the bar. Lisa—that's her name. I've spent a few nights with her. She's a good girl. I saunter over to the chair and when Lisa spots me she jumps off the seat.

"Oh, hi there. Didn't see you come in. Saved your seat," she says as she adjusts her dress to cover the pink latex panties she's wearing. It's a really fucking short dress.

Lisa chews her gum nervously and rubs her hands together in front of her. Sighing, I stroke her bottle-blonde hair behind her ear.

"The gum, Lisa. I thought you broke the habit. *Tsk.*"

Her jaw has been bothering her and her doctor told her to stop chewing gum. When she couldn't stop, she asked me to help give her an incentive, and since then I haven't seen her chew it for months. I enjoy helping people like Lisa, people who need a little *push* to achieve their goals. The kind of help only someone like me can give them.

"It's been a rough week."

When she looks down at her hands in shame and all I see is her blonde hair, pink clothes, and wide hips, I can almost pretend she was someone else I'd like to be with tonight.

"Why don't you tell me all about it, Lisa? And then we'll get you to stop again, won't we? You'll be a good girl for me?" I tip her chin up to look at me.

She has brown eyes and a more angular face than Crystal. Her hair is yellower. She's beautiful, yes, but she's not who I really want. I guess she'll do for the night, though.

"Oh, yes. I promise. I'll be the best girl, I swear." She bounces on the toes of her pink Pleaser heels so excitedly her tits nearly come out of her top.

I can't help but grin just a little at her excitement. Lisa might not be the one for me, but she *is* sweet and tonight I'll treat her right. Well, in the way I do anyway.

"Come. We'll find better ways to use that pretty mouth."

I wrap my arm around Lisa's shoulder, and we head upstairs where I've already booked a room, planning to spend the night away from town as I tend to do on my visits to this place.

However, it turns out I don't need the room tonight. As soon as I close the door to the room and Lisa runs a pink-nailed hand down my chest, I know this night won't end any other way than with me alone. I take Lisa's hand away from my body and ask her about what problems caused her to start her nervous gum-chewing habit again. I let her talk about it until she seems to have worked through her issue, then I give her a kiss on the cheek, claim a stomach issue, and go home.

I can't get Crystal out of my head. It bothers me greatly that she will be with Trig doing who knows what passionate things while I can't bring myself to spend the night with a woman who I know well. But it can't be helped. I'm already in too deep. *Fuck.*

Chapter Sixteen

Trig

The glass misses my face by about an inch max as it smashes against the wall behind me. *Holy shit that was close.*

"You scrawny motherfucker! You think you can just scuttle up and take the only new pussy this town has had in years? You think she wants your pencil dick?" Brutus, the owner of the auto repair shop, doesn't seem pleased that Crystal is going on a date with me tomorrow.

I'm not really sure how he knows, because I didn't tell anyone, and I don't think Crystal did. But I also don't see why it's a problem. It's just a date!

"Brutus! Calm down!" shouts Mary from behind the bar. She owns this place and she's not afraid to mess some people up if things get too rough. "What the hell is going on?"

"This piece of shit asked out the new pie lady and now she's taken for the whole weekend. He knows some of us are older and therefore should get first pick of new women. That's how it should work." He slams a fist against a table, and I cringe.

Wait. I only asked her out one weekend day. Hmm.

"The lady can date whoever the hell she wants. Now, calm the fuck down or get out of my bar." Mary spits her words at Brutus.

"It ain't fair," Brutus throws another glass at my head, which I barely dodge before he heads out the door. *Yikes.*

"Sorry, guys," I say from the corner where I'm admittedly cowering. I'm definitely not a fighter. "I swear I didn't try to provoke him."

"Brutus just sucks," James laughs as he pats the seat of the booth next to him. "Get your ass back here."

The physical education teacher and I were just eating our burgers and drinking our beers when Brutus started screaming at me to stand up. I knew something bad was going to go down. I didn't want James to get involved so I stood up and moved to the side. Then all that mess happened. *Oof.*

"He totally sucks. If he liked her, he should have asked her out. She would have said no though because he's gross, obviously." I take a bite of my burger and a glob of mustard splats onto the front of my white t-shirt. When I try to wipe it away, it just smears further. "Um. Maybe I shouldn't talk about gross. I should know better than to wear white at dinner since I'm such a freaking disaster."

"Yeah, you are. But not like Brutus. You're just a little messy. Gotta have backups." James zips up my black hoodie. "There ya go, all better. No one will know now."

"Thank you, thank you." I laugh. "Now I will just have to remember to bring a hoodie on my date tomorrow I guess."

James sets his elbow on the table and his head on top of his hand, looking at me thoughtfully.

"You really like this girl, huh? I've never seen you nervous about a date before."

"Yeah, I do. She's so sweet. And wow, she's gorgeous. I have this feeling that we're...I don't know. There's a connection there."

My phone buzzes and I quickly peek at the notification. *Crystal.*

"And there she is. Let me check this text really quick."

I pull up my messages to see what she says. *Please don't cancel.*

> *Hey there! I have a little something serious to talk about. Phone okay?*

Oh, shit. I read the message again to make sure I read it correctly. Okay. I guess I have to call her.

> Yep! Let me find a place outside with no Brutus.

> Okay...you do whatever that is then. <3

> Ooh, a heart! :D

"I'll be right back, James," I tell my friend, scooting out of the booth to head outside.

I dial her number and wait while it rings. When it rings more than a few times I start to wonder if she'll even pick up at all. Finally, she does.

"Trig! Hi! Glad you called."

"Hi, Crystal! You said it was important." I try not to sound like I'm panicking, even though I am.

"Yes. Well, maybe. I guess I'll just say it out-right. I took a date for Sunday," she pauses. I can tell there is more to what she needs to tell me, but she wants me to assure her anyway before she goes on.

"Alright. That's okay, I guess." My heart hurts a little, but it'll be fine.

"Well, the thing is the other person is Cliff. I don't want you to be upset with me."

I'm quiet for a good while after that state-ment. *Cliff?*

"Did you hear me, Trig?" she asks. "Are you mad?"

Then I start laughing. I can hardly stop long enough to answer her.

"Cliff? Does he know you're going out with me tomorrow?"

I laugh long and loud before she's able to answer in the affirmative.

"Oh boy," I continue. "And he didn't lose his mind? I can't believe it. This is crazy. Well, don't worry, it doesn't bother me. I'm glad you told me, though."

"I'm glad you got a laugh out of it." She giggles. "So, I'll see you tomorrow?"

"Nothing could hold me back."

Chapter Seventeen

Crystal

Could this be it? Could they be the ones?

It's a beautiful day, perfect for a picnic. The weatherman said it would be chillier, but he was wrong as usual. It's just barely warm this morning, a little cloudy, the type that warms your nose but not your toes. By the early afternoon, it should be heavenly sunshine. I wore a heavy button-up sweater to wait out by my front door, but by the time we eat, I know I'll be in just my sundress.

Why does that make me think of the guys I've chosen to date? One is soft sweaters and cloudy weather; the other is short sleeves and sunshine. Somehow it works. For the first time since Miranda's curse, I'm thinking there's a chance that...well, maybe it's too soon to hope.

There's just been so many things lining up and I can't ignore them. What happened when Trig touched my hand. How I could suddenly hear when I was the pyramid. Two men, that I actually really like, asking me out within moments of one another. Those men being okay with me dating both of them despite them not getting along.

So, while I would normally turn down any date, I've accepted these two. I've got hope.

"Hello!"

Trig's jolly greeting breaks me out of my thoughts. I watch him walk his bicycle up my driveway with a giddy feeling in my belly. Something about the way he looks pushing that blue bike, his cheeks rosy, hair mussed, in a pale-yellow jacket, makes me feel like a young girl again. I can almost feel my dad's eyes on my back watching to make sure this boy doesn't put the moves on me.

But boy, I kind of hope he does put some moves on me.

"Hi there, Trig! You can come park your bike right here, no one'll take it. I'm the only one over here." I look around the corners, smile dropped to give him a look as if we're sharing a secret. "There's all the cameras too, of course."

"Oh, of course." He nods solemnly before breaking out into his signature boyish grin as he settles his bike against the porch. "You do have one fairly close neighbor, though."

"I suppose. I haven't met them though. Don't know anything about 'em." I think back to if I've heard anything from my new neighbor yet but nope, not a peep.

"You don't know?" Trig looks really shocked. "It's Cliff!"

"What? You're kidding me! Well, that's just funny." *Add it to the list of odd things and coincidences, I guess.*

"Yup, he doesn't like living in the town so he's way out here. Lucky grump somehow ended up next to the prettiest lady in the county. Can't believe it."

"Just in the county? It's not a very big county." I raise my eyebrow and put my hand on my hip playfully.

"Well, if I told you that you were the most beautiful woman I've ever laid eyes on—in the whole world—would you have believed me? Even though it's absolutely true?" Trig is standing only a few inches away from me now, close enough for the heat from his body to take away the last remaining chill of the morning.

"I suppose I wouldn't have." I lean just a little closer.

"Well, then you see why I started small. I'll start off with you believing you're the prettiest lady in the county, then pretty soon you'll know as well as I do that no star in space could outshine you."

"You went from the world to all of space."

"I told you, moving up."

Trig steps back from me and I feel the loss of his presence like an ache. Pulling a basket off the backseat of his bicycle with an "Oof," he holds it in front of him with both hands.

"Alright, I'm starving. Where are we headed?"

"Come on back this way!" I lead him around the side of the house and through the tall, wood gate.

As we walk through my large backyard, he's pretty quiet. I can tell by his wide grin and sparkling eyes that he's enjoying all the sights around him. I haven't had much time to work back here since it was chilly when I moved in, and I haven't even been here very long, but I've started planting early-season crops and flowers which means there's a lot of dirt back here. Still, he looks fascinated. When we get to the tree line and start on the path toward the clearing, he finally speaks.

"I have a garden, too, but it's not as big as yours looks like it's going to be. Last year things didn't turn out so great. I got a few tomatoes and some sad carrots. This year I'm going to do better though, I'm determined." He lifts his chin, and I have to giggle. Something tells me this guy has a lot of first-garden-flop-type experiences, but also that he doesn't give up. I do like a positive attitude.

"Well, we'll see if mine turn out alright or not. I'm mostly trying for peppers this year since they've been so dang expensive at the store lately. If I succeed, I promise to make you some salsa." This is a test. If he doesn't love salsa there's no way we can be together. I just love it so much.

"Ooh! I can't wait to try your salsa. I have to warn you, though, I'm a bit of a salsa snob. It's my favorite and I'm rather picky." He tugs the lapel of his jacket with his free hand and shakes his head in a faux snobby manner that makes me snort. Test passed, I guess.

"Oh really? Well, I'll try to be up to your standards then." I tease, smiling back at him as we enter the clearing.

Earlier, I laid out a blanket for us and set out the champagne and orange juice in a bucket of ice next to the glasses. A mimosa can't hurt today when my nerves are jangling like this. Trig sets the basket down next to the ice bucket and then takes my forearm, helping me sit down before he joins me. What a sweetie.

"Alright, let's see what you got," I say with a laugh as I rub my hands together.

"Ah, an impatient one," he says as he opens the basket.

"A hungry one is more like it."

"That I can relate to."

First, he pulls out some plates and silverware, setting them between us. Next, he pulls out a package of chips, followed by a small mason jar of what appears to be homemade salsa.

"Are you kidding me?" I ask, my jaw dropping wide open.

"I told you; I'm a salsa snob. I make it just how I like it. You can try it now, too, tell me what you think." He winks at me, and I can't help but squeak out a laugh.

Next, he pulls out classic turkey sandwiches on a lovely bread that had to have been freshly baked, a zesty pasta salad with lots of fun veggies, and chocolate cake.

"I didn't bring pie—I figured that's your domain."

"I appreciate it." I laugh. I don't wait around, just dive right into the chips and salsa. It's fantastic. "Oh, my goodness. You have a right to be stuck up. Where did you learn this?"

Ruffling his hair, he looks down shyly. "It's not like I made the recipe up, I don't know. Salsa is a cultural thing I'm not even a part of. Really, I'm just mixing ingredients that have been traditionally used together. I just kind of got lucky with the specific distribution of—"

"Okay, I get it, Trig." I cut him off before he can continue to babble. I know a nervous babbler when I encounter one. "Did you make any of the rest of this?"

Taking a bite of the pasta salad, my eyes go wide. The veggies are so crisp and fresh, and the pasta is perfectly tender but not mushy. Everything about it is wonderful.

"All of it, yeah." His face turns pink as he rubs the back of his neck.

"How the heck did you learn to cook so darn good?"

"My mom was a terrible cook when I was little. She got sick when I was older and decided before she died, she was going to learn to do it well, and she wanted me to learn too so I wouldn't be useless in the kitchen. I did okay, but after she died, I kept learning until I was good enough to feed a family, should I ever have one. I certainly don't feed myself well though." His nose wrinkles as he cringes in embarrassment. "It's basically gas station food most days."

"Oh. Oh, that's not good." I suck air through my teeth and shake my head.

"I know. I'm just so focused on other stuff and it seems such a waste to make a lot of food for one person. But I think we should stop talking about how unhealthy I am, and we should talk about you instead."

"Terrible segue, but I'll allow it," I laugh.

"Sorry, sorry. We just have talked a lot about me and not about you. I want to know more about you." He smiles at me, and I can't help but blush a little. He's so dang cute.

"Well. Besides the fact that I like salsa and pie, I like things that aren't food."

"Wow, really? Amazing!" He slaps his hand to his chest in faux shock.

"It's true." Okay. What can I tell him? Now he's going to expect something real. "I really like animals. When I was young, I went to veterinary school but decided it wasn't for me. Too hard to see the animals in pain. I'm just a wuss, I guess."

"It's okay to have a soft heart. Not everyone can be the strong one. Besides, there are lots of ways to be strong. I bet you have plenty of them." He fiddles with the hem of my dress, and I wonder if he even realizes he's doing it.

"Well. I guess I've always been good about staying calm in emergencies. Like if there's an oven fire, I never panic, I just put it out. Or when someone needs help, I just do what's got to be done. Does that count as being strong?" I twirl the ends of my hair nervously.

"It certainly does. If there wasn't someone like you in a crowd when something bad happened who would be calm enough to call 911 or give CPR or something? We need people like you. So, you may not have been able to do vet work, but it doesn't mean you're weak." His smile is ridiculously bright now that the sun is fully out and shining on his face. "I love animals too, by the way. I have a cat named Pytha, after the Pythagorean theorem."

"That's so nerdy. So, so nerdy." I can't help but laugh.

"Well, what's your dog's name?" he asks, affronted.

"His name is Plato. A perfectly normal name."

"Plato is a nerdy name too. There are so many nerdy facts about Plato I don't even know where to begin. Did you know he thought that each element was sort of represented by a shape? He thought my favorite shape, the tetrahedron, was fire." He continues to mess with the hem of my dress absentmindedly as we talk.

"That's beyond nerdy that you even know that." I raise my eyebrow.

Add the fact that his favorite shape is apparently the one I become every night to the list of "coincidences."

"I only bring it up because I have a new favorite shape now."

"Ok?" What a weird thing to say.

"Mhm. Yours." His eyes drift down to where he's rubbing the hem of my dress. Letting go of it, he slowly, so slowly, slips those two fingers under the hem to stroke the bare skin of my thigh.

I inhale sharply half in surprise at how forward he's being and half because of how good his touch feels. Each pass along my flesh feels electric, hot, like whips of flame intended to please, yet still so gentle.

"That was the weirdest and nerdiest way to try to get in my pants I've ever heard," I try to sass back, but the way my breath shudders out of me betrays me.

"I'm glad you're not wearing pants then, so I don't have to worry about getting you out of them." He catches the edge of my skirt on his thumb and pulls it up with the stroke of his fingers, revealing more of my thighs. "Is this alright?"

His eyes flit to mine, seeking permission. I don't exactly know what he wants, but I know whatever it is I want it too. I nod, waiting to find out what happens next.

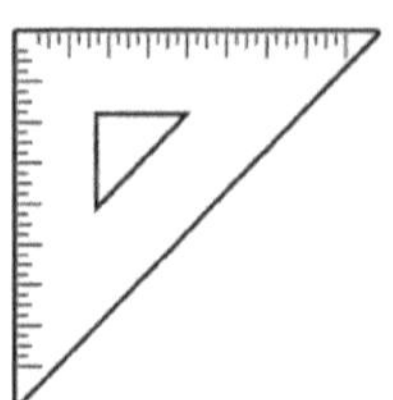

Chapter Eighteen

Trig

Wow, I didn't expect to move this fast. I don't know what came over me. As soon as I accidentally touched her thigh, it was like my head went blank and then all I could think about was touching her more. And she's *letting me*. This is amazing.

When she nods, I lift her dress a little bit more, just a fraction of an inch at a time. I want to give her time to stop me if she wants to, and admittedly I'm enjoying the reveal. Continuing my perusal, I find a tiny freckle on the side of her right thigh. Pale stretch marks softly crawl up the sides of her inner and outer thighs, reminiscent of the ghosts of vines. I want to trace them all with my tongue.

Finally, I see a peek of yellow satin panties, just the tiniest bit where her legs are first pressed together. Dropping to my elbows to get a closer look, Crystal gasps and squeezes her thighs tighter together. Looking up, I meet her nervous eyes again.

"Crystal, if I'm moving too fast, it's okay to tell me to stop. Just say so." My voice is raspy but still sure.

"No, it's fine. I promise. It's just that I haven't dated anyone in a long time, let alone...*been with* anyone." She looks embarrassed, so I figure I might as well tell her my truth too.

"Crystal, it's been over seven years since I've been with a woman. Five since I went on a date and that was a disaster. Trust me, I'm not judging." Propping myself up on just one elbow, I lay my head in my hand and continue, "I'm not the ultra-suave heartthrob you think I am."

Some of the nervousness leaves her eyes as she replies with faux sincerity, "Oh, okay. So sorry to have misjudged you."

"Common mistake, I'm sure." I nearly laugh, but that fiery feeling is still burning too hot in my belly.

When Crystal catches the heat in my gaze, her giggling slows, and her look begins to match mine. Getting to my hands and knees, I crawl the last few inches to her, then take her face in my hands.

Our kiss is slow, languid, decadent. Her lips are soft and plush, her tongue nimble and somehow moving perfectly in sync with mine. It's the best kiss I could ever imagine.

Rather than pull away from the kiss, Crystal places her hands on top of mine and lies back on the blanket, bringing me down with her. I keep most of my weight off of her but can't help grinding my aching cock against her center as we kiss.

When she wraps her arms around my neck, I move my hands back down to her skirt, lifting it further. Finally, I pull away from the kiss to look at what I've revealed, seeing tiny yellow panties with lace trim at the top. Something about them is perfect for her, but I need them to be off immediately.

Hooking my fingers under the sides of her panties, I silently seek permission again. She sits up and kisses me hard, putting her hands on mine to help me tug the underwear off of her. They slide down smoothly as we kiss, her hands following mine the entire way until they're off. She finally pulls her mouth from mine, lying back down on the blanket.

Her dress is hiked up around her waist, her shoes still on, but everything between us is spread out obscenely bare and wide before me. *Smooth*. I wondered in the shower what her cunt would look like and now I know. It's shaved smooth and glistening wet with arousal already.

Running my hands along her inner thighs, I spread them wider, enough to fit myself between them, before finally just yanking her toward me and hooking them over my shoulders. Crystal yelps, then giggles and I can't help but laugh back. Her joy is infectious. I want to give her more. So, I bring my mouth to her beautiful, wet cunt and I lick it long and firm with the flat of my tongue.

Crystal's giggles stop then, turning to deep sighs. One of her hands goes to her snowy hair, running her fingers through the silky strands with the rhythm of my licks. The other hand pulls down the top of her dress so she can squeeze and fondle her small breast as I pleasure her. The sight is enough to make me groan against her in lust. I *need* to see this woman come.

Carefully, I insert two fingers inside her. I pump them in and out, listening to the obscene squelching sounds as I watch her pull out her other breast and squeeze both of her nipples hard. I notice the green glow coming from—

The green glow?

My eyes reluctantly move away from the sight of Crystal's hands to mine, and I realize I can see my fingers. All of them. Everywhere I'm touching Crystal is transparent and glowing, just barely, a soft greenish blue. I sit up and stare as I wiggle my fingers a bit inside of her, gasping as I see the action perfectly.

"What's wrong?" Crystal asks, breathless, as I slip my fingers out of her.

"You're, um, just look," is all I can seem to get out.

When Crystal lifts the part of her skirt blocking the view of her lower body and sees the...*issue*, she screams.

"Hey, don't freak out, it's okay." I try to soothe her by wrapping my arms around her shaking shoulders in a tight hug. The hug doesn't seem to work because she shrieks, long and loud.

"It's not okay! My pussy is invisible!"

"Okay, I mean, that's weird. But we can figure it out. I'm sure there's an answer." I run my hands over her hair, trying my best to comfort her, though I don't really know how to do that. I mean, I would be pretty freaked out if my dick disappeared.

"There's only an answer if Cliff can do it too, maybe, but otherwise I don't know! Who else has ever had this problem? How would I even begin to figure out why—"

"Whoa, hold on."

I step back from her, keeping my hands on her shoulders as I look into her eyes. *This just keeps getting weirder.*

"Did you just mention Cliff? I think that's a little weird to talk about other men when I just had my face between your legs. Maybe we need to set some boundaries."

"Oh gosh, I'm sorry. Okay." She places her hands on top of mine and squeezes them, taking a deep breath. "I didn't mean to say that out loud. It doesn't mean I was thinking of him like that. There's just this problem I have that I think I need both you and him to fix. But I can't really tell you about it right now."

"I think you kind of have to. I just saw my fingers wiggle around while they were inside your body. And I can still see a glow coming from under your skirt, so I kind of want to know what's going on." My eyes go wide as I have a sudden thought. "Are you an alien?"

"What!?" Crystal steps backward, pushing my hands off of her shoulders. "What the heck made you think that?"

"The glowing crotch."

"Oh. Yeah. Well, no, I'm not. It's a—this is going to sound dumb but just believe me—it's a curse." She bites her lip and folds her hands in front of her waist, wringing them nervous-ly.

"I guess I kind of have to believe you. But how did you not know it was going to happen? You know you're cursed so you should know what's going to happen." My brow scrunches in confusion.

"Well, the sorceress who put the curse on me was a little vague. There is kind of a lot to it and some I'm still finding out it seems."

"Sorceress?" I scratch my head as I pace back and forth like the confused idiot I am. "I'm having a lot of trouble with this. What else is there to this? And what does Cliff have to do with it?"

"This is going to take a while to explain. Why don't we sit down."

Chapter Nineteen

Crystal

The last of the champagne mixes with just a drop of orange juice in my glass. I toss the bottle aside and chug the drink back. No point in trying to be classy when I've just laid out the most ridiculous story of all time in front of this man.

"So, then that means you *love* me? And Cliff? That seems pretty sudden." Trig crosses his arms as he slouches over his bent knees.

"Well, I don't know what to tell you. I'm assuming this curse can sniff it out before I can or something. I mean, I think you're pretty great, but I've never been in love, so I don't know what it feels like. It probably feels like more than one date, though." Dang, I wish there was more champagne. This is so awkward.

"I think you're pretty great too." Trig plops his head on his crossed arms and carefully watches me in silence for a moment before speaking again. "Can I see you as a pyramid?"

I wasn't expecting that one.

"Oh boy. I guess. Just be careful, it's dangerous out here at night, if you don't know the path well. You could trip and fall or get lost or encounter an animal or something." *Or see me like that and never want to talk to me again.*

"I'll be fine. I promise. You're not glowing anymore, by the way." He nods at my crotch area, and I sigh in relief.

"That's good. I really didn't want a permanently neon coochie."

"Neon coochie could be a good band name." Trig perks up with a silly, lopsided grin.

"You are such a dork. You're cute though."

I brush back the hair that has fallen across his brow so I can see his eyes better, watching his pupils grow larger as they meet my eyes in return. I can't help but kiss him.

This kiss is soft, a caress. I'm not sure if he still really wants me after all he's learned, but when he kisses me back hard, I know he does.

He lifts me by my ass and pulls me into his lap. We kiss rough, wet, for a long time. He unzips my dress, pulling it off of me so I'm fully nude on top of him when he lays his head on my chest and groans.

"You're perfect, Crystal. Better than anything I imagined."

"You imagined me, huh?" I whisper into his ear.

"Oh yeah," he rasps against me.

"Let me see you. Please," I beg as I lean away from him. He tries to follow my body, but I push him back.

"Alright, alright," he says reluctantly as he begins to remove his jacket. His fingers are nimble and quick and within seconds he's topless, his strong, lithe torso bared before me.

I run my hands down his chest, and his stomach until I reach his belt. It's simple enough to undo the belt and then the button of his pants while I watch the speed of his breathing increase. Lifting onto my knees, I undo his zipper and slide his pants down, letting him kick them the rest of the way off.

He has a lovely cock, thick and already leaking pre-cum for me. I can't help but lean in and lick that drop off the tip. Trig hisses and lifts his slim hips, running his fingers softly through my hair.

"So beautiful. I can't believe it. You're fantastic," he breathes out lovely compliments as I run my tongue along his length, wrap my lips around the head of his cock. When I take him all the way into my mouth, hitting the back of my throat then letting him past even that, his words turn into strangled moans.

Wind whips around us, cooling my heated flesh. The sudden reminder that I'm outside, fully nude, with a cock in my mouth in the bright sunshine makes my stomach flip with nerves. Then it makes me ache lower with something else.

I release Trig from my mouth with a *pop* and a giggle, but keep my hand on him, stroking slowly. He runs his hands up and down my thighs, watching me as I do so and we both inhale as my hand becomes translucent, glowing at the spot where it meets my normal body. I'm glad there is a glow in the places where the see-through bits meet the opaque parts, otherwise, there would be a pretty nasty view of my insides. Whatever the glow is seems to block that, thank goodness. Either way, it's still strange to look at.

"Your hand—" he starts but I cut him off.

"Just ignore it. Just feel me. Feel the sunshine on your skin. Anyone could stumble into these woods and see us. How would that feel, Trig?" I throb between my legs at the mere thought of it.

"Um, it makes me nervous. I don't want to get into trouble."

Aww, he's such a good boy.

"What if Cliff accidentally wandered too far off his property? And he saw me riding your cock? How would you feel then?"

The way he stiffens in my hand and his hips jerk tells me all I need to know.

"You'd like that, wouldn't you? Admit it. You'd like him here, with us." I wouldn't have thought it at the start of the day but...yeah, there's something there.

"Yes. I would." I expected a sort of dirty shame on his face I could tease him with but there is none. *He's thought of it before.* "Fuck.

Please, Crystal, I need to be inside you right now."

"Well, since you said please."

I line myself up with him and slowly sink down, watching the points where I touch him go invisible as I do. The sight is alarming but somehow becoming more and more arousing. I can see a sort of vague outline of myself, it's not one hundred percent invisible, and there's the glow, of course. But other than that, it's his cock fucking up between my legs now, bent and squeezed by my invisible force. It's so strange and neither of us can take our eyes off of it.

"This is so weird. But so hot. What the fuck?" Trig manages to mumble out between his panted breaths.

"I know. And you feel so good. My brain is about to shut down in confusion and just let my body take over."

"Sounds like a good idea to me." Trig begins to thrust up harder.

My sweet man presses his thumb to my center and after some awkward searching finds my clit. It's strange to see him rubbing circles in what appears to be thin air next to his thrusting cock but *fuck* it feels fantastic. He curves when he enters me; I never really thought about how much a cock has to do so when it enters a vagina. *Hey, look at me, learning about my own body.* He glistens with my wetness, getting increasingly wetter as I do. It's impossible not to watch what's happening between us. The sight only increases the intensity of the feeling.

After a couple moments I clench hard around him and come with a silent scream, my eyes shut, and my mouth open wide. I can't see what's happening below but Trig's "Whoa," tells me it must look pretty interesting.

When he comes inside me shortly after, I do see it, and I am fascinated. I love watching the cum spurt out of him in rivers, only to get squeezed, squished, and swallowed by my body. By the way his eyes grow huge, and his mouth gapes at the sight, I think he finds it pretty exciting, too.

I slump down to lay my head on his chest, listening to his heart beat ridiculously fast, wondering what other parts of me are invisible right now that he was too polite or distracted to mention. I suppose it doesn't matter. It'll go back to normal. Right now, this moment is too good to ruin with pointless questions.

Trig wraps his arms around me, and we lay together quietly for a long while, enjoying the sounds of the forest and the lovely feel of the sun. Eventually, we see ants all over the food we forgot to pick up and laugh as we scramble to clean everything and check to make sure we don't have bugs on us. We don't, thankfully, but I am invisible over most of my front, unfortunately. To our relief, after about ten minutes it goes away. Once we're all dressed, packed, and I'm opaque, we start walking back to the house. Trig turns to me, a questioning look on his face.

"How are you going to get Cliff to believe you? Just walk up to him and put his hand up your—"

"I'll figure it out. Don't worry about it," I cut him off. I really only need to share so many details between dates.

We get to the fence, and I stop, turning once more to Trig.

"So, you'll come back here and see me change tonight? Are you really sure?"

"Yep! And don't worry, I'll be careful." He wraps his arm around my shoulder and kisses my temple. "I promise."

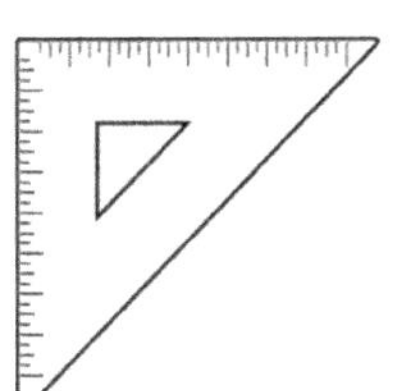

Chapter Twenty
Trig

When midnight hits, Crystal looks to the sky and in a flash, she's gone. In her place is a beautiful pyramid of...well, crystal.

My breath rushes out of me and my knees go weak. Even after everything I've seen and heard today, this is just a lot to handle. I drop to the ground and sit, legs crisscrossed, and stare at the sight before me.

It's beautiful. Or should I say *she's* beautiful? I'm not really sure in this context. I feel a draw toward...*her*. Like I should go and touch the smooth sides. Like I *need* to touch them.

But then, I hear a rustling some distance away, a sound like running. *Shit.* Crystal and I didn't plan for this. Panicking, I take off in the opposite direction as quietly as I can, diving behind a bush. I watch between the branches, remaining as still as possible, as I wait for who-ever is coming to pass by.

Except the person who comes out of the trees doesn't pass by. They stop. It's *Cliff*. And he's...what the fuck?

It takes me a second to fully comprehend what's happening because it's just *weird*, but it's true. Cliff appears to be jacking off onto Crystal's pyramid shape. Holy shit. Does Crystal know about this? I mean, I knew Cliff liked rocks and gems, but I didn't know he liked them *this* much.

Then again, I *did* feel that strange pull toward her. Maybe he feels the same thing and I could have been the one fucking a rock right now.

It's kind of hot the way he's clearly conflicted about what he's doing. He keeps looking away and frowning as if he wants to be anywhere but here. At the same time, when he looks at her his eyes light up and there's this expression like real adoration. I've never seen him like this, not even close. I can't tear my eyes away.

Soon enough his face scrunches in what ap-pears to be the world's most reluctant orgasm, and the pyramid is splattered with cum. He takes a hand towel from his pocket and wipes it up before quickly running back the way he came. I wait a bit before stepping back into the clearing so that he won't hear me. I don't get too close to Crystal; I don't want to get drawn in with whatever magic drew Cliff in.

"Hey Crystal, if you can hear me, I hope you're okay. That was fucking weird. Does that always happen? Was I supposed to see that? I'm so confused. Uh, I'm feeling really weird right now—like I should come closer—and that's freaking me out. So, I should probably go. I'll text you. You look really pretty, by the way. Very shiny. Okay, bye."

I take off back down the path, so distracted that I forget to turn my flashlight on, and I stumble on a stone, falling and turning my ankle. *Fuck.* It doesn't break or anything, but it hurts and I'm probably going to have a little limp for a couple of days. Annoying. Crystal is going to "I *told you so*" the shit out of me. *Ugh.*

I limp back to my bicycle and ride back home. When I pass Cliff's house, the lights are off. I can't tell if he's still out, or if he's sleeping, and

I wonder if he's guessed anything at all about Crystal.

This is the weirdest day I've ever had.

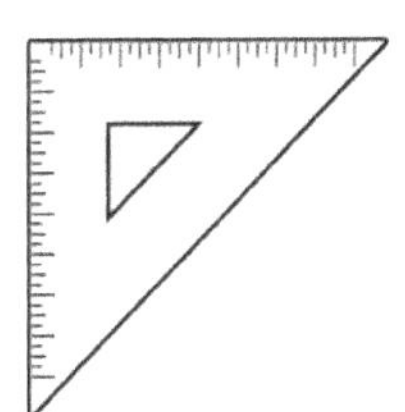

Chapter Twenty-One
Cliff

Once again last night, I ran. Once again, I felt drawn to the clearing. I'm ashamed of what happened there. I stayed awake far too late because of it and this morning I'm now tired. Which is unfortunate as this is the day of my date with Crystal.

I have an extra cup of coffee this morning to ensure I am as awake as possible. The worst thing I could do is yawn and have her think I find her boring. Certainly, Trig did no such thing yesterday.

Trig. I must stop letting him get into my head. This is my date with Crystal, not his. I won't let him ruin it. Sipping the last of my morning beverage, I clear my head of all negative thoughts.

Coffee consumed, Trig out of my head, I leave my home and head to Crystal's.

When I arrive, I intend to knock at her door like a gentleman should, but she is already outside waiting. She looks glorious. Her white hair is down in soft curls around her shoulders. A pale green summer dress highlights the adorable wrinkles of her knees.

Who knew I would ever find knees adorable?

She scurries to my vehicle before I can even get out to open the door for her and hops in. Her smile is wide, her lips glossed and pink. I want that gloss left in rings around my cock.

"Hello, Crystal. Are you well?" I ask.

"I'm great! We still going out for breakfast?" she replies in her perky way.

"Yes. Please buckle your safety belt." I've known too many lost to accidents and I refuse to move until she's secured.

"Yes, sir!" She salutes before buckling in. *Sir. Fuck.*

"And we're off. I hope you enjoy Spanish food. A traditional Spanish restaurant opened in the city and it's quite delicious. I think you'll like it. You seem like the type to try many types of

things." I offer her a quick smile before return-
ing my attention to the road ahead of me.

"Oh, I love trying new things. I admit I haven't
had a lot of traditional Spanish food, but I'm
sure I'll like it because I've enjoyed what other
new foods I have eaten quite a bit."

I'm glad she enjoys trying new things. That
gives me hope for other parts of the relationship.

"Do you go to the city a lot?" she asks.

"Only on the weekends. To visit friends," I
quickly add. I'm not quite ready to tell her the
real reason I visit the city so frequently, and it's
not *really* a lie anyway.

"Oh, that surprises me."

"Why? You don't think I have friends?" Well,
that's a bit insulting.

"No! That's not it! You just seem more like
the type that likes to, I don't know, spend his
time alone most of the time. Like reading or
something. I'm not even sure what I thought!"
She stumbles through her words.

"Technically, I do. I spend all of the weekdays
and Sundays, as well as most Saturdays, alone.
But I'm not quite what everyone in town seems

to think I am. I know everyone thinks I dislike people. I admit they're not entirely incorrect, but I do enjoy the company of some; you for example. I'm particular about the company I keep, but I do keep company nonetheless." I hope that settles things.

"I get it. Honestly, I don't really have any friends. There are some issues I have that make it difficult to keep people close. You and...well, you know who, are the only people I've let this close in a very long time. So please don't think I was judging you when I thought you were a loner. I wouldn't judge you either way. I like you." She sets her hand on the arm I'm using to shift gears and even through my cardigan I can feel a bolt of energy go through me. I like her so, so much.

"Thank you, Crystal. We're here."

We go into the restaurant and take our seats. It's a cozy new place run by a friend of a man I spent a night with once. I'll leave that minor detail out of the conversation. Crystal and I order our drinks—her orange juice and my coffee.

I tend to have a difficult time trying new things. Thankfully, Spanish food was common in my household alongside the unpalatable traditional American beige mush, and there are a few things I can comfortably enjoy. Crystal orders huevos rotos and I order tortilla de patata. While we wait for our food, we talk more.

"Tell me about yourself, Crystal. What do you do when you aren't running the shop?"

"Oh, I like to garden. I have a dog named Plato and take him for walks around. I like hiking in the woods. I like reading."

"What sort of things do you enjoy reading? Perhaps we enjoy some of the same things."

"Oh, well, probably not." She blushes and looks down as she takes a sip of her orange juice.

"I read quite a variety of things. You may be surprised." It's true, I read anything from scientific articles to silly crime fiction novels.

"Unless you like reading about sexy, sentient pillows or mushroom fairies, I'm not sure we have much in common." She starts to giggle increasingly hard until I can't help but join in.

"Indeed, I don't believe we have that in common. Perhaps you could lend me a book or two one day. I would be willing to try anything."

She smiles at me then, her eyes crinkling at the corners in the sweetest way. I can imagine her then as an old woman and the thought is not unpleasant. The breath is knocked out of me for a moment. I realize I truly am falling for her, and so quickly.

"I like that you're so open-minded. You have to admit you're a bit stuffy most of the time, so I'm pleasantly surprised."

"I do admit to being rigid about things. I have my reasons. Some of those reasons will never make sense to most people and I understand that, but I'm not close-minded. I think you'll find me a lot more willing to experiment in some areas than you'd think." I raise my eyebrow just slightly to see if perhaps she might catch a hint. By the blush that hits her cheeks, I can tell she does.

"That's good to know," she replies, her voice a bit lower than before. "I'm quite willing to experiment as well."

"I'm very pleased by that, Crystal."

Just then our food arrives, and the rest of our conversation revolves around her work at the shop and my work at the museum. Learning more about her daily life is exhilarating. She's so passionate about her work, and when she talks about it her face lights up, her energy infectious. When she listens to me talk about my work, I can tell she's truly engaged and not bored. She asks questions and doesn't zone out like most people, which is important to me. All in all, it's a wonderful breakfast.

When we're done and I pay for our food, despite her trying to insist she pay for half, we drive back, continuing our talk about our professions. As we get near to the town, however, Crystal interrupts me.

"Can we go back to my place? I'd like to show you something." She looks a little nervous and I can't help but raise my eyebrows. I didn't expect her to invite me back to her house for sex but it seems that's what she's doing, if her expression is anything to go by.

"That would be fine."

After parking in front of her house, we go inside and are immediately greeted by the biggest dog I've ever seen in person, which Crystal takes outside into a fenced area before coming back inside alone.

Crystal gestures for me to sit on her sofa and she joins me, wringing her hands nervously in her lap. Things are awkwardly quiet for a bit and I'm not sure if I should say anything or wait for her, but then she finally speaks.

"I've never touched you skin-to-skin, so I'm not sure if this will work. I hope it does or I'm going to feel real stupid. Anyway, I'm going to take off my dress and I just need you to touch me some different places and see if anything strange happens." She bites her lip and stands up, unzipping the back of her dress.

"I'm confused. What do you mean by strange?" I'm not unhappy she's undressing, of course, but this is very odd.

"You'll know it when you see it." She huffs out a little laugh and shakes her head as the dress drops to the floor.

Crystal stands before me in nothing but a pair of green lace panties. Any concerns I have about the situation disappear as I take in her soft thighs, full hips, and perfect breasts.

"Okay. So, just touch me however feels right, I guess. How do you want me to stand? Or sit?

I don't know." She poses awkwardly with her arms out.

I shake my head. Something comes over me and before I can stop myself, I find my mouth moving.

"Lay across my lap, face down." *Fuck.* She's going to tell me to fuck off.

She doesn't tell me to fuck off, instead nodding before doing as I asked, draping herself over my lap. For a moment I'm frozen, my regular confidence out the window, hypnotized by the perfect roundness of her ass. Then the spell is broken.

"Good. Now, I simply do as I please?" I twirl a lock of her soft hair in my fingers as I wait for her answer.

"Yes," she breathes out. "Whatever you want."

"Very good."

Slowly, I let my fingertips drift down her spine, enjoying the sight of her back arching when she's tickled by them. I get to the hem of her panties and pause.

"I'm going to remove these now."

"Yes, Sir," she replies. *She knows what I want.*

"Such a polite girl."

I drag the underwear slowly off her ass revealing evenly tanned skin underneath. She must tan nude. *Tsk.* Naughty girl. Between the lips of her cunt, I can see the telltale glisten of desire. Excellent.

"Anything I want."

I run the flat of my hand firmer up the delicious roundness before me then over to position my hand over her tailbone. I drum my fingers there for a moment, drawing out the tension.

"Hmm, I wonder. Crystal, are you a good girl or a bad girl?"

Crystal lifts her head to look at me, surprised.

"Um, I think I'm good. I don't hurt anyone." Her brows scrunch together in confusion.

"True. You are dating two men who despise one another, however. Does that make you a bad girl, Crystal? I want to reward you for being so sweet and polite by making you cum on my fingers. Then again, this ass would be perfect for a spanking. So, I need to know. Good or bad?"

I lightly slide my middle finger down her center. She shudders and sighs.

"Why not both?" she shakily replies.

With a grin, I lean over and whisper in her ear, "I like the way you think."

Stroking her snowy locks, I take in the jasmine scent of her shampoo before pressing my cheek against hers. "Did you kiss him, Crystal?"

The shaky breath she lets out gives me my answer before her words do. "Yes."

"Did you do more than that?"

"Yes. A lot more."

Fucking Trig.

"Did you suck his cock, Crystal?" I can barely form the words, my jealousy so full in my throat.

"Yes."

"That makes you a very bad girl. A bad girl with a very dirty mouth. What do you think happens to girls like you?" I rub my hand in massaging circles on her ass, giving her a pleasurable hint.

"Naughty girls get spankings, sir," she whispers.

"That's correct. Now, hold still."

My hand flies up, then down, smacking her ass. In all my years in the lifestyle I've been a part of, I've never seen such a perfect jiggle as the one I'm watching now. It takes everything in me not to push her to the floor and fuck her into tomorrow. Instead, I softly rub the place I just spanked, soothing the area.

"Alright?" I ask quietly.

"Y—yes," she stutters out.

"Good. Now, Crystal. One more thing. Did you fuck him?" *Please say no.*

"Yes. I did."

I sigh in displeasure as I rub the other side of her behind. "Are you ready for your lesson?"

"Yes, sir." She arches her back so she's pushing against my hand. *Naughty little minx.*

Slap! A second spanking, followed by another soothing. Crystal moans and writhes on top of me and I feel as if I could burst.

"You did so well. You answered all my questions truthfully and took your punishment without complaint. I think you deserve a treat for being such a good girl. Don't you?" I slip two fingers down her center until I meet the incredible wetness there.

"Yes. Yes, please."

"You even say please. So polite. Good. Now you can come on my fingers. Maybe next time you can come on my cock." *Fuck fuck fuck fuck, please.*

"Yes yes yes please yes," she whines.

I move one of her legs over just slightly to make room for my hand. When I slip my middle and ring finger inside her, facing downward so that my thumb can press against her clit, I find that she's absolutely drenched.

"So wet for me." I pump my fingers in and out a few times, searching for her special spot, and when she gasps, I know I've found it. I begin to rub her clit along with my massaging. "Such a perfect cunt. Do you think about me inside you, Crystal?"

Running my other palm along her stretched-out throat, I wonder what it would be like to squeeze it as I fuck her—if she'd enjoy it. Perhaps another time.

"Yes, sir. Oh, that feels so good." She shivers and I watch as her skin turns red and blotchy. Such a beautiful sight. I move my fingers quicker, keeping my motions smooth and watching her breathing and twitching for signs of when to further increase my pace.

"I'm so glad to hear that. Now, I'm going to need you to come for me very soon." I feel her pulse race in her throat as she moans, lost to the throes of passion, and I make my final push. "Come now."

Within a few seconds Crystal stiffens, a single shout leaving her frozen body, before she collapses loosely over me, still gyrating slowly against my hand. She lets out a soft, pathetic mewl as I remove my fingers from her and I can't help but chuckle.

"Don't worry, there will be plenty more of those for my good girl soon enough. Now lick them clean for me." She eagerly sucks her fluids off of my fingers as soon as I put them into her mouth. "I'm sorry to break it to you, but nothing strange happened like you said. Though I'm still not sure what you were expecting."

I lift her up, intending to hold her against me, but instead release her in shock. I barely catch her before she hits the floor, though I have no idea what to do when she's in my arms.

"It appears I spoke too soon."

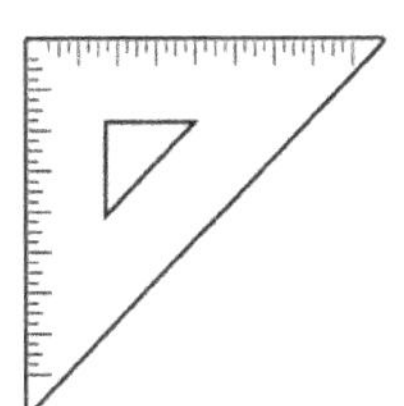

Chapter Twenty-Two
Crystal

From the chin to the coochie I'm invisible. On one side anyway. Got a nice glowing layer in between, like a radioactive sandwich cookie.

Cliff sits on my sofa, back straight, hands on his knees. I stand before him, still nude, letting him look me up and down. He sure looks for an awful long time before finally he clears his throat and pats the seat next to him.

"Sit. Put on your dress. We clearly have some things to discuss."

When I'm dressed and sat next to him, he does the one thing I really wouldn't have expected from him: he takes my hand in his. I look into his eyes and see amusement there, not fear or judgment like I worried. Shoot, I don't know why I worried so much more with Cliff than I did with Trig. Maybe because he's so serious. But now I feel kind of guilty about making assumptions about him.

"Here I thought I'd tried everything. Never been with an invisible woman, though." He grins and strokes my cheek. "Why did only some of you turn out like this? And how long does it last?"

"I'm not really sure why only some does, or why it never happened before I met you and Trig. It seems to last anywhere from a few seconds to about ten minutes as far as I can tell. It's real finicky, it seems."

"Never happened before Trig and me? What's different now?"

He combs his fingers through my hair as we speak, making me feel like melted butter. This man really knows how to use his hands.

"Well, there's this curse..."

A little bit later, when I'm done explaining the whole curse thing, Cliff is back to sitting the way he was, hands to himself. He suddenly looks a little green and I know it's not from me because I'm back to normal now.

"Cliff? Are you okay?" I touch his elbow carefully so as not to freak him out.

"You said you turn into a pyramid of some sort at night? In the clearing behind this house?" he asks in a faraway voice. "The clearing not far from my very own property?"

"Yes, the pyramid is some kind of glass or gem or—"

"Fluorite. It's fluorite." He cuts me off before swallowing hard. He looks at me and I notice the strangest thing on his tanned cheeks. He's blushing! "I've seen the pyramid, or you I suppose, there before."

I think back to the last couple nights when I'd had a...visitor and I feel a blush creep onto my cheeks as well.

"I don't suppose you were there last night, were you?" I ask, unable to look him in the eyes.

"Yes, I was. My apologies. You must understand that I couldn't–You see, I–" The normally stoic man stumbles over his words.

"It's okay. I don't think you could help it. It's just more proof that we're on the right track." This time, I'm the one who takes his hand in mine. "I just don't know what I'm supposed to do now."

"I don't know either. This isn't something that one can really research, I suppose."

"No, not really." I laugh. "I do think we'll all have to get together and talk about it though. We'll figure this out together."

"Absolutely not." Cliff yanks his hand from mine. "I will have nothing of our relationship to-*gether* with Trig. Things are to be kept separate."

I bristle at his sudden harsh tone. "Well, Cliff, if this was a normal situation I'd agree, but it isn't. I think it's pretty clear we have to work together."

"I said no." Cliff stands, straightening the cuffs of his sweater. "You have no idea what you ask of me."

"This is my life and you're more concerned that he played a game over a decade ago. That seems—"

"You think this is because of the game? I suppose you would. That's what he thinks." Cliff flops back down to the sofa and pinches the bridge of his nose. "But no, that was only the last straw for me."

I slip into the spot next to him and tentatively lay my head on his shoulder. "Tell me what happened. It seems like you need to talk about it."

"Perhaps I do. I never really have, after all." Cliff wraps an arm around me and pulls me close. "Alright. It started when we were kids."

Chapter Twenty-Three
Cliff

We were close the moment we became friends. We did everything together for years. But Trig wanted to be physically close as well, despite my aversion to touch as a young child. He'd run up to me and ruin a project I was working on when he should have kept back, or he'd invite me to sleep over before he'd finished cleaning his room despite knowing how much it bothered me to be in a messy house. It drove me nearly insane and only made me want to be farther away from him.

But when he was troubled and wanted to be held, such as when he woke from a nightmare, I couldn't turn him away. Because he would never turn me away when I was upset or in trouble. So *eventually, I became used to his touch. Eventually, I even craved it despite my dislike of it.*

As we got older, those cravings were for a different, more intimate sort of touch.

Trig was popular. Handsome, friendly, intelligent, kind. He fit in everywhere and never had a problem finding a date. I was...awkward. Girls would mostly date me to get close to Trig or to hang out with their friends on double dates with us. It wasn't a big deal to me really; I had no interest in anyone that way. Well, anyone other than Trig, even though he didn't know it.

When senior prom came around, I finally decided I was going to tell him the true extent of my feelings for him. We were sitting in his room, the one I'd just spent all afternoon cleaning yet again, discussing this and that's when I just decided to go for it.

"Would you go to the prom with me?" I forced out.

"Yeah, duh. We need dates though." He tossed a baseball up and caught it over and over, a thoughtful look on his face, as I sat there confused. "Who should we ask?"

"We could just go together, is what I meant. You and me. As dates." My throat felt like it was closing by the time I finished that statement, but it was done, finally.

Trig paused and looked over at me before replying, "Nah, they wouldn't let us in, you have to have real dates. All the teachers already know we're just friends, we can't trick 'em." He went back to tossing the ball. "Maybe we should ask Amanda and Maria. We had fun with them the other night, right?"

My heart was crushed. I was so far out of his idea of a romantic partner that he couldn't even consider I would ask him out. Not even when I made the words as clear as anyone could. That nearly destroyed my confidence in dating for years. Once I got it back, I decided to keep any whisper of my love life away from Trig to protect my own heart.

There was no more double dating. I sought out my own comforts but found I had difficulty in any sort of relationship where I felt...vulnerable. I didn't want to be hurt again, and touch was complicated for me. It still is. When a short-term lover introduced me to a different type of relationship dynamic, it finally helped me take my mind off of the hurt of Trig's dismissal.

But anyway, after that crushing blow, I decided not to let him take advantage of me; not to let him push my boundaries anymore. If his room was a mess, I simply left and told him to call me when it was clean. If he destroyed something I worked on, I made him compensate me for the repairs. Once I started doing that, I began to realize how often he was absolutely fucking up everything, expecting too much from me.

Yet, I still gave him everything when he needed it. When he climbed into my window, heartbroken, one night after Amanda dumped him, and he wanted to sleep next to me, I let him. When his dog died and he wanted to hold me for hours and cry, I let him. When he wanted to go to the same college and move in together, so we didn't have to be apart, I went along with it. I had no control when it came to him.

Finally, I decided I wanted to break away, I wanted to live for myself. Not for my parents, not for Trig, for myself. I had rushed through school and gotten my degrees faster than anyone thought possible of me. I was going to get my dream career, make a new life. Have some fucking control for once. And he wrecked it. He ruined it.

It's not about the one time. It's about everything. I loved him. I did everything for him. And he couldn't give me one thing for myself.

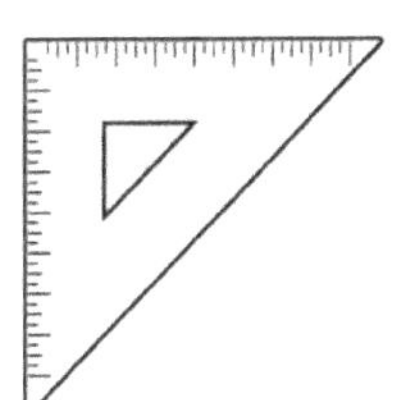

Chapter Twenty-Four
Crystal

"So, you see why I don't want to share a love life with Trig. Not after the hurt. Not after the heartbreak." Cliff presses his head against mine. "But I'll do it for you. You don't deserve to be under a curse just because I can't get over something that happened when I was just a boy."

We sit quietly for a moment, and I can't help but feel overwhelmed by the weight of his admission. It must have been very difficult for him to open up like that to me. I've never been in his shoes and don't even know where to begin to help him heal. But I do want to help him. If things work out the way I think they could, then we'll have time to work on things together.

"Oh, hon. I can see why you'd be hurting. Thank you for sharing that with me. I'm honored to know that you trust me with your feelings. Knowing you're going to work through all of that history to help me with my curse means so much. Cliff, I promise things will be okay. You're such a sweetie." I can't help but squeeze him tight.

He scoffs. "Rarely has anyone referred to me as anything like a 'sweetie' but I suppose I'll accept the compliment."

"You'll take it, and you'll like it." I laugh.

"Oh, I will? And what will you take?" There's no laughter in Cliff's voice, but I can sense a hint of playfulness beyond the rough edges.

"Hmm. I don't know, what do I need to take?" I sit back and tap my finger to my lip in thought.

"I know what you need, *sweetie*." Cliff snatches my hand and presses it back against the wall behind my head. Slowly he leans in near to my ear, close enough that his lips brush my skin as he speaks. "Now let's see how much of it you can take."

With one fluid movement, he scoops me off the couch and stands. When I begin to make a noise of protest, he tosses me over his shoulder as if I'm nothing more than a sack of grain, lifts my skirt, and bites my ass cheek.

"Ah! My ass!" I yelp.

"Point me to the bedroom or I fuck you into the carpet, your choice, but the bedroom will save you from the rug burn. I can't promise it will save you from anything else." He traces a finger around the light bite mark, and I break out in goosebumps.

"Out the door to the right," I manage to squeak out.

"Good girl."

A moment later, I'm unceremoniously tossed onto the pink sheets covering my queen-sized bed. I lay breathlessly on my back and watch as the man I thought was just a bit of an uptight nerd turns into something that is very much *not that.*

He removes his cardigan, setting it neatly on the chair that faces the end of my bed. Next, he begins to unbutton his shirt and the moment the top of his chest is revealed my eyes nearly bug out. *He's covered in tattoos.* Every piece of clothing that he removes had been hiding more artwork.

They're beautiful. Dark caverns full of mineral formations. Mines of crystals and gems. Mountain peaks capped in snow. Volcanic eruptions. The earth from his feet to his shoulders. It seems like it should be a strange mishmash, but it's not. Everything has clearly been well thought out and carefully placed. All the art is fantastic, and the execution is flawless. Only one piece doesn't fit in with the rest.

"What's this?" I point to the area near his heart left open with nothing but a simple design. All that's there is the outline of a triangle, inside which one corner has been blocked off into a square shape. There are letters on the sides and corners of the shape.

"It's a right triangle. It was my first tattoo. I thought getting something related to trigonometry would be a terribly clever way to punish myself for falling in love with my particularly straight best friend. Now, is that all you're going to say when I'm nearly naked in your room? How disappointing. *Tsk*."

"Nearly! Not completely!" I hug a pillow to myself and can't help but giggle. This man is so weird. Such a huge romantic, a big geek, neurotic as fuck, and dominating in the bedroom. I can't tell what's coming next. *Except hopefully me.*

When he strips off the final article, his underwear, he looks at me and raises one eyebrow as if to ask, "Are you satisfied now?" Oh boy, am I satisfied. The man is *packing*. And *pierced* all down the shaft.

"How the hell am I supposed to take all of that inside of me?" I unwittingly breathe out.

His lip curls up at one corner as he replies, "What was it you said? Oh yes, 'You'll take it and you'll like it.' Now take off that dress and spread your legs, we need to stretch you out."

I find my mouth has suddenly gone dry when I try to respond so I just nod instead. The zipper goes down quickly, and I fling the dress to the floor. Cliff sighs as he sees the green fabric in a crumpled heap, before leaning down to pick it up. He watches me judgmentally as he carefully folds the garment before placing it on top of his own meticulously folded clothes.

"Don't tell me I have to train you not to make a mess. I'd hoped you'd come housebroken already." He shakes his head at me. I shrug apologetically, still unable to form words.

Wanting to distract Cliff from my misdeeds, I spread my legs before him. The trick works. His eyes immediately flick to my center where they stay. His head tilts to the side as he inspects my form, his hand running languidly over his massive cock. Finally, he crawls onto the bed and presses my thighs open farther, slowly getting closer to my aching cunt.

"I'm quite happy you aren't invisible here yet. You're a wondrous sight to behold."

The compliment makes me want to close my legs in embarrassment; I always get embarrassed by compliments. I force myself to keep them open, however, and let him continue what he's doing. Without preamble, he slips two fingers deep into my slippery center and groans.

"You're almost ready for me as it is, *sweetie*." He chuckles at the mocking pet name. "I'm going to have to make you come again to really get you prepared. I shouldn't be too rough with you, it being our first time and all."

He kisses down my thighs until he's nearly against my lower lips. "I can't promise I'll be so *sweet* next time."

In a move much faster than the languid kisses he had been bestowing upon my thighs, he begins going down on me and it's unreasonably, impossibly, nearly unbearably magnificent. *Fuck.* I don't even realize he has four fingers inside me when I come only about a minute after he starts. When he sits up on his knees, licking those fingers one by one, I can only stare at him in shock with my mouth hanging open.

"Alright then," is all he says before he falls on top of me, pinning my arms above me and trapping my legs to the sides with his.

His mouth crashes to mine and he kisses me hard, ruthlessly, forcing me to taste my own arousal on his tongue. He nips my lips, pressing hard enough to leave bruises. He literally *growls* against my neck, as if he can't even stand having to abide by human decency standards. I could nearly come again from him grinding his pierced cock against my clit alone as he ravishes me with these animalistic kisses.

"I want to tear you apart, Crystal. I've wanted to do terrible things to you since the moment I saw you in that shop. It's taking everything in me to hold back. But I will. For now. For you. You're too sweet, too good to hurt, even though I can tell you want it." The ache in his voice as he presses his forehead against my chest is powerful.

"I don't want what you think I want from you at all, actually," I whisper. His head lifts, his eyes look apologetically into mine. "Cliff, I *want more.*"

"*Fuck,*" he grinds out between his teeth.

That's all I get before he flips me over onto my belly, ass pulled in the air. Before I can react, he plunges deep into my pussy in one hard, fast movement that leaves me gasping and crying out. He drives hard into me, relentlessly, his huge cock spreading me open like I've never been before.

"Oh fuck, it's too much," I whine, feeling as if I'm about to be torn in half.

"No, it's not. Your cunt is perfect for me. My sweet little slut takes both her men in her pretty pussy and loves it, don't you?"

Oh fuuuuuck. I clench harder around him, barely able to reply. "Yes, I love it. I want you both. Fuck me."

Cliff wraps my hair around his fist and yanks me upward until we're flush against one another, him still driving into me. He drags his teeth down my neck as if a threat.

"Would your *Trig* like to see you covered in another man's marks? Would he like to know what a slut you are for me? Would you tell him how far up your cunt my cock went? Hmm?" He tugs my hair back harder, making me cry out and moan.

He thrusts up inside me until he hits the deepest point, the spot that hurts to touch but that I love to feel regardless. He hits it over and over until I feel tears form at the corner of my eyes and my legs shake with an impending orgasm.

"I asked you a question. Will you keep us a secret or will you open your dirty little mouth after you suck his cock again and tell him what we've done?"

"Whatever you want. I'll do anything you want," I reply in a high voice, barely able to control my body.

"Don't tell him anything. Unless he asks." He forces me down onto all fours, my face pressed against the mattress, and ruts into me like an animal. "I've never felt anything like you, Crystal. You were made for me. You're mine. He's only borrowing you."

I want to protest the possessiveness, but at the moment he feels too fucking good, and I can't stop myself from coming hard around him. I scream into the pillow below me as all my tension finally lets go in one muffled burst of release.

"That's it, that's my good girl. Squeeze my cock."

As I come down from the intense orgasm, he rolls me over onto my back, my limbs loose. He presses my legs up and out, creating a shallow entry for him that lets him hit that deep spot again, making me cry out between gritted teeth.

"Enough," he growls, wrapping a hand around my neck. "It's my turn. You'll be silent unless you're milking my cock, understood?"

I nod as best I can with his hand on my throat. He lets go and the air whooshes out of me. My head spins and I see my thighs, my pussy, my tits that he's squeezing start to go invisible. Cliff looks down and huffs out a laugh when he sees it but doesn't stop what he's doing. In fact, he goes faster, pressing his thumb where my clit would be without having to search for it even though he can't see it. All we can see is the incredible bulk of him being squeezed by my inner muscles over and over. His piercings flash in the light as they push me closer to insanity, the way they push through the textures of my insides. I keep my moans in and manage to stay quiet, until I feel him fumble his movements just slightly. I know he's close.

I break apart once more as he does, squeezing him as he spurts ropes of cum inside me. I let myself shout as my tight cunt milks every drop from him. He groans and kisses me lazily as he finally slows.

We wrap our arms around one another and breathe each other in. Under the sweat from our lovemaking is the scent of nice shampoo, books, and laundry detergent. It's a stoic kind of scent you wouldn't expect from a man who fucks like a beast. Then again, he's also a man who wears cardigans that cover his tattoos every day, only chooses the classic apple pie, and meticulously folds his laundry. This man is a puzzle, and I intend to spend my days solving him.

As I ponder my future, my mind begins to drift. I hear soft breathing next to me, and I smile when I realize Cliff has fallen asleep. When I glance at him now, I see how young and innocent he looks, and my smile breaks open wide. *Sweetie.* I don't want to bother him, so I don't budge from my spot. He wore me out, so I let myself relax with my eyes closed, accidentally falling asleep for too long.

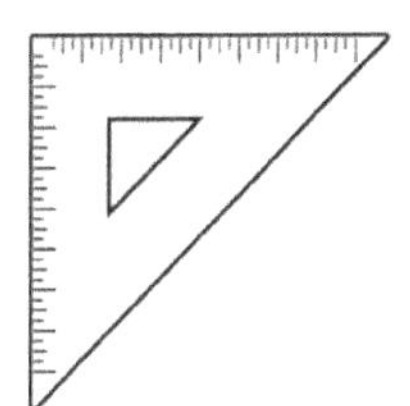

Chapter Twenty-Five
Cliff

Mmm. I stretch in the dark, then wrap my arms around my sleeping date. She's snoring softly...

Snort.

...and occasionally she's snoring loudly. It's adorable. It's quite dark in here and I wonder what time it is. I know it was already deep into the afternoon when we fell asleep, but it can't be that late.

It is that late.

"Crystal, wake up. Now." I shake her shoulders hard.

"Huh? What's wrong?" she mumbles, rubbing her eyes.

"It's seven minutes to midnight is what's wrong. I believe you have some business to attend to and a long way to walk."

"Oh, shit." She tosses back the blankets and stumbles out of bed.

"Here." I toss her the green dress she was wearing earlier, and she scrambles into it. I get myself into my pants and shirt. I'll get my underclothes and cardigan another time.

We jog out the door, only stopping to put on our shoes and lock the door, then head to the woods. There are a few stumbles along the way in the dark, but we finally make it there in one piece. However, we don't make it exactly to the center of the clearing before midnight hits, and I'm standing far too close to Crystal when the clock strikes twelve. When she changes suddenly, my leg gets caught *under* Crystal.

"FUCK!" I scream into the woods.

I can see my shin under her gentle glow, smashed into the earth. Thankfully the ground where we stopped is soft and I seem to be in a more "leg pressed into the earth" and not "leg snapped off" situation. It's the part under my knee, not my entire leg, so I have some freedom of movement via my hip. Not that it really matters when I'm trapped here. *Shit.* What am I going to do?

There's only one person I can call. Damn it. *Trig.* Reluctantly, I use my shaking hands to pull my phone from my pocket, and I pull up the number I thought I'd never use, the one I thought about deleting a million times, and dial it.

"Hello?" His voice is scratchy with sleep.

"Trig." Mine is hoarse with pain. "I need your help."

He wakes up when he recognizes my voice, "Anything. Tell me what you need."

It takes nearly twenty minutes for Trig to arrive even though he actually drove this time. He hates driving, but he did it. It's just a long walk with the limp I didn't know he had.

"Okay. I have no idea what to do. The pyramid is making me feel, uh, *weird* but I'm trying to ignore that," Trig starts babbling and I know I need to cut him off.

"Good. Pulling your dick out wouldn't help right now," I snap. "I believe we need an ambulance but I'm afraid they will need some equipment to lift this, and then people might still be here when Crystal changes back to her human form. I can see some of my leg, but I need you to get a better look and tell me how much blood I've lost. If I can risk staying here until sunrise, I will."

"Oh, man. Okay. Um, it looks, uh, bloody. But it's sort of pushed into the grass and dirt and you have pants on most of it so I can't tell how bad. I think your circulation is probably fucked though. You have to get this taken care of. I'm not a doctor but it just doesn't seem like a good idea to stay like this."

"Fuck. Trig, I don't want them to hurt her. Isn't there a way we can move this?" I grit my teeth as a lance of pain shoots through me.

"It's a massive rock that I'm surprised didn't actually cut off your leg entirely with its weight so no. I mean it's really heavy. Actually, hmm. Maybe I could tip it over with—"

A darkness seeps into the edges of my vision, and I begin to feel very tired.

"Hey, Cliff, sit up. Don't pass out." Trig is shaking my shoulders. The darkness recedes.

"Alright." I run a hand over my face and find myself to be ice cold. "I'm cold, Trig."

"Oh shit. Cliff, I'm gonna call an ambulance, okay?" Trig's voice is tight with panic.

"No, Crystal."

"It'll be okay. We will figure something out. I can't lose you."

"You already lost me long ago." A sob breaks from my chest, and I cringe in embarrassment.

If you'd have asked me yesterday if I would be spilling my emotions in front of him, I would have laughed in your face, but now…now I don't have the will to stop. Too much pain at once, too much fear. It's no longer possible to hold it all inside, as hard as I try. I'm too exhausted to hold up these walls. I'm in pain, I'm tired and I have been for so, so long.

"Cliff, please. Don't say that." Trig puts his forehead on my shoulder and I'm too weak to shake him off.

"I loved you and you turned me away. You rejected me. Then you ruined my life." The tears are flowing freely from me now as I pour my heart out. I can't stop these words, despite my mind screaming at me to end this.

"You loved me? I rejected you? What do you mean?" Trig's voice is full of hurt and confusion, and I could almost believe that lie it sounds so honest.

"I asked you out to prom and you turned me down. Maybe you didn't even realize I was asking but that hurts just as much. You never even considered me as a candidate for a lover." Sobs break from my chest one after the other. I can't even feel the embarrassment anymore over the pain.

"Cliff. I didn't realize. And I never considered it because I never thought you'd want an idiot like me." Trig falls back on his heels, his face fully serious and dark for once. Tears fall from his beautiful gray eyes, and I wish I could wipe them away. "All I've ever wanted was to be close to you."

I think about our lives, everything passing in a flash. Every moment that he lost or fumbled just to be near me. I sob harder.

"You left me all alone. You were all I wanted, everything I needed, and you left me. I didn't know what those feelings were and I'm sorry. I don't know why it took me so long to realize it, but I love you and I can't lose you. Even if you still hate me and tell me to go away every day, I just need you near me. Please don't go away." Trig curls up into himself and cries in soft sobs.

The beautiful man before me becomes, for a moment, the boy I knew so long ago. The one who came to my bed when he couldn't sleep for fear of monsters. When he was heartbroken. When his dog died. He always came to me.

My heart shatters harder than any bone ever could.

"I never hated you. I never could. Why do you think I took this job? It's no coincidence that I came back here. As much as I wanted to be away from you, I couldn't. Not really." I hiss as pain shoots through me again. "Call the ambulance. Promise me you'll protect Crystal somehow. Then we'll...we'll figure out where life begins after this."

I rub my eyes to push away the darkness that keeps insisting on leaking into the corners of my vision.

"Okay. Okay, I will." Trig calls the emergency number and gives them directions.

It's fairly easy to tell them how to get here once they know where Crystal's house is, but it will still be at least ten minutes for them to arrive. I just have to stay awake that long. It seems a monumental task.

"Stay with me, Cliff. Who will finish setting up the benitoite display if you don't?" Trig wraps his arm around my shoulders and sits next to me.

"No one could do it as well as I, and you know it," I reply. And it's true, damn it.

"See? Stay awake." Trig smiles

"It's very difficult." I find myself slurring my words a bit and begin to worry.

"Shit. Um." Trig holds me tighter as I begin to slacken in his arm. Then he wraps his other arm around me and holds me to his chest. "Okay, so how about this?"

He kisses me.

I wake the fuck up.

His arms are wrapped tightly around me, supporting me, and I can't move my own arms to stroke his soft hair like I want to. But I can feel his face, his skin just very barely rough with the day's stubble, against mine. His lips are warm and supple. When he lightly licks my own lips I open them for him, too stunned to return much more movement than that. He kisses me passionately regardless. He's careful, sweet, everything I knew he'd be. If I had enough energy of my own, I'd eat him alive. For now, I accept his offer and return it in kind.

Using the only energy I have left, I lean forward until the back of his head is pressed against the pyramid. I pull my arms from Trig's grasp and press them to the stone on either side of his face.

Then I lurch forward as the stone disappears.

Chapter
Twenty-Six
Trig

C rystal has been asleep for weeks. As soon as Cliff and I both touched her in her pyramid form she poofed, right back into her regular form. Since then, she's been unresponsive. The doctors couldn't find anything wrong with her, she's apparently just exhausted. I took her back to her house once the hospital released her and have been taking care of her and Plato.

Cliff had to stay in the hospital for a while because of his messed-up leg and the shock. He hasn't wanted to see me. That hurts pretty bad. I thought things would be different after what happened between us.

Today, he calls unexpectedly and tells me to meet him at Crystal's house. Obviously, I'm going. I even take my car to make sure I get there on time.

When I pull up, I see Cliff waiting there with his crutches, his lower leg in a cast. He's healed really well and really quickly so far. I swear he's good at everything.

"Hi Cliff! How's it going?" I wave as I exit my car.

"I'm out in the hot sun, standing on crutches. That's how it's going. Let's get in already."

What a grump. Gotta love him.

"Okey dokey!" Jogging up to the front door, I open it with the keys I snagged from Crystal before the ambulance took both of them away that night. I try to help him up the stairs, but he pulls away and makes it up himself without any trouble.

When we get inside, he makes a wobbly bee-line for Crystal's room, and I follow after him. I'd follow him anywhere. He stops in the doorway and looks around the room with a stern look on his handsome face.

"You kept everything tidy."

"Yeah. I tried," I reply nervously. I really did try.

"Good." He hobbles over to the chair next to Crystal's bed, unaware that I'm bursting inside with joy at his praise.

"She still hasn't said anything?" The only time we've spoken has been his texts asking me if she's said anything. He hasn't been able to move around well enough to visit her on his own until now I guess, so he's needed me to keep him up to date. If I asked him anything else, though, he just didn't reply.

"Nope. She's looking healthier, though, and she's moving around a little more in her sleep." She looked a little gray at first but now she's got her lovely pink cheeks back.

"Well, that's good at least." He watches her as she snores softly on her pink pillows, a hint of sunlight coming in through the thin curtains leaving golden strips on her skin. "I love her."

Those three words hang in the air between us despite the incredible weight of them. There are infinite possibilities there, how I could react, how things between us can change. In the end, there's really only one way it can go.

"I love her, too."

I sit on the floor in front of Cliff, my knees pulled to my chest. He towers over me like this, a king and his supplicant. I beg him with my eyes for a touch of his grace.

"Then I suppose we have some things to discuss. More than Crystal, I know." He swallows hard and looks away from me. The room is silent for a long moment.

"You left me alone again. For weeks. Why?" I can only whisper my question.

"I had to think. It wasn't... I didn't mean to... I'm sorry." He still won't look at me. He swallows hard again.

"Please don't do it again." My question is small and soft. If I ask louder and bigger I'm afraid it will scare him away.

He swallows and nods before looking at me with his dark eyes, and I break.

I spring forward, reach for his face, and kiss him with everything I have. There are tears running down my cheeks, but I don't care, and I don't think he does either. Some situations allow for ignoring vulnerabilities.

Cliff pulls me away by my hair, making me gasp. He doesn't look angry, his eyes are hot with lust and his breath is quick, but I still look back at him with confusion.

"What now? What do you want, Trig? When she wakes up, and I feel it in my heart that she will, what will you choose?" His eyes move quickly, searching my face for answers before my mouth can move. They don't need to search long because my answer is right there.

"We don't need to choose, Cliff. There's more than one way to live a life. Why choose? What good would that do?" I gently untangle myself from his fingers and lay my head on his chest. "We can have it all. The whole freaking triangle."

Cliff is silent for a moment before he begins to stroke my hair. My whole body relaxes with his blessed touch.

"If you're sure, then I have no trouble with it. I've been in much stranger relationships with people I care for much less. There was the dominatrix and the clown I spent a month in France with, for one. It was all fun and games until her ex-girlfriend, the astronaut, began making trouble during Slappy's balloon time. I'll never eat freeze-dried ice cream again." After he tells that bombshell of a story, he continues stroking my hair in silence.

As soon as I can pick my jaw up off the floor, I turn my head to look up at him. "You're joking, right? You're the guy who won't ride a city bus because sometimes the numbers on the seats are peeled off and it makes you uncomfortable to see them missing. And you went to France to date someone named Slappy the Clown?"

"Slappy didn't like the bus either."

"Is there—are there more things I don't know about you?" My brow scrunches in disbelief. He's gotta be fucking with me.

Cliff's lip lifts to one side. "So very many things. Would you like to discover some of them?"

He lifts me by both sides of my face and the grin he gives me tells me that *fuck yes* do I want to know them.

"I very much would like to, yes, please."

"Such a good boy, so polite."

My cock begins to swell at the praise. *Yep. That's the stuff right there.*

"Now, sit back."

I do as he tells me and watch as he unbuttons first his cardigan, then his shirt. He removes both, leaving him in only his white undershirt. I haven't seen him dressed in this little clothing in many years, and I have to say that I don't remember him being this fit. Or maybe he was but I just wasn't looking at him this way. Either way, he *definitely* did *not* have all of the tattoos.

"What the fuck?" I whisper under my breath. He might as well have just turned into a unicorn.

He grins wider as he pulls off his shirt, revealing even more tattoos on his gorgeous torso. He's so beautiful, not some sculpted muscle bro, just lean and toned. Someone who got their body from working out for their health and not their vanity. I want to kiss every part of him and thank whatever god or force of nature brought him to me.

I tentatively bring a hand up and touch one of the tattoos on his stomach, smiling when his abs twitch. I trace along the myriad geographical formations in wonder. This must have taken so long and been so much work and pain, and he's kept it hidden. Such a shame. It's then that I see his chest. The tattoo that doesn't belong.

He sees me see it and sighs.

"Yes, I got it because of you. Don't make a big thing of it."

"I'm going to make a big thing of it. I'm totally making a big thing of it." I smile so wide I'm sure my face will split in two.

"Don't make me put you over my knee," he mumbles.

My mouth goes dry and my hand stills. Cliff looks at me and a darkness crosses his face. *Fuck.*

"Would you like that? Crystal did. You would, wouldn't you? How lucky of me to have not one but two naughty little playthings." He begins to stroke my hair again.

I try to reply but I can't seem to form words.

"Nothing to say? What a shame. One of my playthings has a useless mouth. *Tsk.*"

His hand slides from my hair to my jaw, and I gasp as his thumb forces my lips apart, pushing into my mouth.

"Suck."

I suck. I suck like my life depends on it.

"Eyes on me," Cliff's quietly commanding voice brings me out of my thought spiral. "Don't let your mind wander again. That won't do when you're with me. You'll give me all of your attention, or we're done. Do you understand?"

He drags his thumb from my mouth, wiping my saliva on my chin as he goes. When he brings his hand to his own lips and licks where I'd just wet it, my own hands shake.

"Yes. Yes, I understand. I'll pay attention."

"Good. What else do you want to know about me, plaything?" He goes back to petting my hair and I shiver at the pet name.

I reach a shaking hand to his belt buckle and pause half an inch above it, waiting. As much as I want to make a joke or shy away, I keep my eyes on Cliff's. He nods, granting me permission to continue.

With a bit of awkwardness, I undo his belt and the zipper on his well-tailored, dark gray trousers. I can't pull them all of the way off because of his leg, and I don't want to make him lift uncomfortably twice, so I tug down his pants and underwear at the same time.

My eyes open wide at what I see right in front of me. Cliff was always a little shy. He would get into a swimsuit or whatever, but he wasn't the type to go skinny dipping. I had no idea he was hiding a fucking monster down there. And it's pierced. *What the fuck?*

"Who even are you? You fuss over the tiniest scratch yet here you have metal jammed through your-"

"Let me explain something you've never understood. There is a difference between things I have control over and things I do not. This difference is what matters in most cases. If I am cut by some random, jagged piece of metal, many unfortunate possibilities could arise, none of which I have control over. If I find the most reliable and clean piercer in the state, use the best aftercare, and know the risks, then I have control. On top of that, it feels fucking amazing. Do you understand, Trig?" He cups my jaw and leans closer to me.

"I think so, yeah." I nod as best I can in this position. "It feels good? Like how? When?"

"Like if you were to suck my cock, for example." He runs his thumb across my lips again, eyes focused there. "Would you like that? Have you ever sucked cock, Trig? You have such a beautiful mouth, so soft, it would be a shame to waste it."

I swallow nervously before shaking my head. "No."

"No, what?"

"No, I've never..." I clear my throat and sit a little straighter. "I've never sucked off anyone before."

"Are you going to suck my cock, Trig? Tell me. Say it." The heat in his eyes is absolutely scorching and it makes me want to touch myself. I have a feeling that wouldn't be welcome right now. This is all about Cliff.

"Yes. I want to." I sit up as straight as I can in this position. "Please let me suck your cock."

My cheeks are flaming hot. *Am I really going to do this?* Cliff sits back in his chair, settles his arms on the armrests, and grins. His cock stands proudly, waiting for my mouth. *Fuck yes, I am.*

"I just want to warn you, I don't know what I'm doing." My hands are sweating, and I lick my lips to keep them from going dry.

"Put it in your mouth and figure it out." He chuckles.

Right before I can take him into my hand, however, he grabs my wrist to stop me. He leans over and whispers in my ear, "We can stop anything at any time, and I will never hold it against you. I will never leave you again. I love you. If something makes you uncomfortable just stop or say no. Tell me you understand."

"I understand," I whisper back, my heart singing like a bird in my chest.

"Carry on then."

He sits back and as he does, I wrap my hand around him, still awed by how thick he is. I shuffle forward and nervously open my mouth, letting my tongue flick out first over the crown as I pump my hand up and down once. I take a moment to see if I can handle the taste and decide that yes, it's not bad. A bead of pre-cum appears and with some anxiety, I lick that up next. Tastes weird, but not bad. *Okay, I can do this. Let's go.*

I try to remember what I've liked that's been done to me, what I haven't liked, and the things that felt good that I wish would have been incorporated by past lovers. I mix these together and start to use them on my best friend.

Or, more than best friend, I guess. Either way, I'm sucking his cock now. And it's pretty fun.

I start to use both hands because he's got a lot of area to cover. He seems to like it when I take him deep because he grabs my hair and pushes me down. It's hard for me, so I gag sometimes, but I keep trying my best. Using my tongue and my lips, I play with those piercings. The sounds he's emitting make me think I'm doing pretty well.

"Fuck, you feel so good, plaything," he rasps out. "Let me give you a rest. Just sit like this and open wide. I'm going to fuck your sweet face, and you can just relax."

Say what?

"Um, okay?" I don't really know what he means, but I'll do whatever he wants—he's my Cliff.

I open wide and look up into his slightly vicious grin. He positions himself over me and aims his cock at my mouth. *Oh, okay, fuck my face, I get it now.*

Cliff groans as he sinks slowly to the back of my throat. When he hits there, I gag, and it feels like he can't go any farther.

"Relax. Just relax. Let me do the work. You only have to open up."

I focus on his dark eyes as I ease the tightness in my throat, feeling the choking sensation as he passes into it. His eyes shut tight for a moment as he stills where he is. Then he pulls back out. Pushes back in.

It's not long before he's brutally thrusting in and out of my throat. Spit is running out of the corners of my mouth, tears out of the corners of my eyes, and my cock is so hard I'm afraid I'm going to come in my pants. All of a sudden, he pulls back just slightly, and I feel the pulsing of his cock, followed by the spurt of his cum hitting the back of my tongue.

I swallow it down, trying not to gag at the new sensation. It seems like he comes forever, but eventually, he finishes, dropping back into his seat, and tugging me up with him. He holds me against his bare chest, and I can tell his heartbeat is just as fast as mine. I crawl up to it on his bare thigh, the one that isn't attached to a broken leg.

"Thank you for that. You played along so well, and you looked so fucking good doing it. I've wanted you so long and you were even better than I imagined. Are you okay with everything? Feeling alright?" Cliff scratches my back and the eyes I'm looking into now are nothing but warm concern and care, nothing like the sex god from two minutes ago. Still just as gorgeous though. *How did I never see it before?*

"I'm good. I think I have some feelings to work through because all of this is new to me. Just...all of it. But I liked what we did. Being with you."

"Good. I'm so—Crystal?"

My head pops up in confusion, my brow pinched in concern. He's so Crystal? Huh? Then I see him looking over at the bed. I turn my head to see what he's looking at and find big sapphire-blue eyes staring back at me.

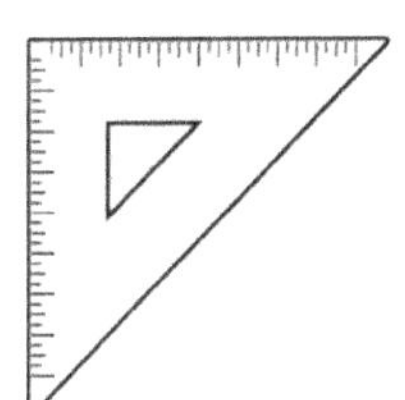

Chapter Twenty-Seven

Crystal

"You're awake!" Trig exclaims, a huge smile on his reddened face. My face would be red too if it took the pounding he just did. *Wow.*

"Crystal, I'm so happy to—" Cliff pauses and looks down at his undressed state, Trig on his lap. He frowns. "Apologies for my current state of undress. Trig and I had some things to work through."

"Mmhmm," is all I can reply to keep myself from giggling.

"Um, were you awake for a while?" Trig asks, his smile suddenly gone.

"Mmhmm," I repeat. My shoulders shake. It's getting too hard to hold in the giggles.

"Oh god. Why didn't you say something?" Trig covers his face and drops to the floor, curling into a ball.

Cliff pulls up his bottoms and puts on his undershirt. "She clearly didn't want to interrupt what had already started. Crystal is a good girl and knows better than to interrupt me when I'm busy. Right, sweetie?"

"Yes, Sir," I purr back. He looks me up and down with a saucy little smile that tells me he's going to want to reward me for being a *good girl* later.

"Do you hate me, Crystal?" Trig asks from his fetal position on the floor.

"Wait what? You're actually upset? Oh baby, no, I thought you were just being dramatic. No, I don't hate you." I toss aside my blanket and kick my feet over the edge of the bed.

"Trig, we talked about this. Crystal is fine. Sit up and look at me. I'll explain it so you'll understand." Cliff says.

Trig sits up and the both of us watch as Cliff tugs down his undershirt to expose the triangle tattoo on his chest.

"Points a, b, and c. All together, we make abc. Crystal and you are ab. Crystal and I are ac. You and I are bc." He lets his shirt go and relaxes back into the seat. "There are different combinations but we're all a part of the same shape. Understood?"

Trig and I both nod. We all take hands in a circle and smile at one another. We're a little weird, and we've got a lot to learn, but it's going to be so much fun.

My stomach rumbles. "I think I need some food."

"Probably. I wasn't able to give you much more than soup when you were out," Trig says.

"How long was I out?"

After the guys fill me in on what I missed, we eat and then I go outside and play with Plato for a while. Soon enough it's dark, and I'm really excited about finding out what's going to happen at midnight. They said I haven't been turning at midnight, but now that I'm awake again who knows? I'm crossing my fingers this curse is over, though.

While we wait for midnight, we watch a few old movies that Trig left here to watch while he was taking care of me. There's this half animated-half live action movie from the eighties that I haven't seen in ages and I'm absolutely absorbed in it when it's almost time to go.

"Hey, time to stop watching that rabbit and get hopping." Trig jokes and I snort.

"Terrible joke, but you're right. Let's go."

Trig and I trudge down the path until we get to the clearing and wait. We left Cliff behind because it would be rude to make him hobble through the forest on crutches.

It's a full moon, so my whole everything is very much on display in the bright lunar light when I get undressed. As twelve hits, I place my arms to my sides, look up to the sky, and...nothing.

I wait a few more seconds in case my clock is off but nope, nothing. No change. The curse is broken. My heart starts racing as a smile crosses my face. I feel dizzy with relief.

"Hey, what was that part of the curse about you'll still be transparent or something?" Trig asks.

"She said '*You'll still be transparent on the full moon*' or something like that. Why?" I ask, now suspicious.

"Just look at yourself," Trig says, exasperated.

I raise an arm to my line of sight and yelp. A second arm has me dropping to the ground. I look at my legs and screech.

"Is it my whole body?" I shout.

"Yeah. You're all invisible. Well, like how glass is invisible. So not like 'The Invisible Man' invisible where there's nothing. I mean there's clearly a shape of you, but that's it. Just a shape." Trig sets his hand on my shoulder.

I stare ahead at my toes, which look like perfect little glass sculptures, and wiggle them. At least they don't move as stiff as glass. I feel physically the same, I just look crazy.

"Well, at least it only happens on the full moon," I mumble. If I don't try to find an upside to this, I'm gonna lose it. "You think we can go back to the house? I really don't want to stay out here. If someone spots us I can, uh, pretend to be a statue or something."

"That is a terrible plan but yeah, we can do that. Come on, get dressed, and let's go. You can take my hoodie and put it on. More coverage."

"Thank you, hon. Now let's go find our angle c."

Not long after, we make it back to the house without anyone spotting us, thankfully. When we get to the living room and find Cliff sitting in my reading chair, looking through one of my smutty books, I have to clear my throat to get his attention.

"Cliff! We're back."

"Oh, apologies. I was absorbed in this story. I can see now why you read these sorts of things. He really has pumpkin spice latte-flavored ejaculate? Intriguing," Cliff says while still looking at the pages. "You must share more of your favorite books with me."

"CLIFF!" I shout. "Pay attention!"

His head snaps up at the same time I lower the hood of the sweatshirt I'm wearing. Cliff blinks slowly several times before setting the book on the table next to him.

"Are you that way everywhere?" he asks.

"Yes. I think it's the part of the curse about me being transparent on the full moon. Hopefully, that means I'll be fine in the morning, but for now, I'm all the way clear as glass."

"Fluorite." Cliff corrects me. "May I see?" He begins to stand but winces when he puts too much pressure on his bad leg and sits back down.

Trig closes all the curtains and locks all the doors in the house as I undress for Cliff. When I'm naked again, I do a spin for him, watching as his eyes open wide in awe.

"I've never seen something so beautiful. You're like a living statue of the clearest glass, or water given form. Do you feel like yourself?" His voice is full of wonder, and it makes me feel less awkward about my appearance.

"You tell me," I say with a small huff of a laugh as I sit carefully on his good knee and wrap my arms around his neck.

Cliff's gaze heats as he wraps one hand around and under me to squeeze my ass. I can't help but giggle and squirm.

"Just as soft and spankable as I remember."

As Cliff leans in to kiss me, Trig comes back into the room and interrupts.

"Oh, I'm sorry. Should I go?" he asks, wringing his hands nervously.

"Trig, why would you go? No offense, but I just saw you with his dick in your mouth a few hours ago." I can't help but laugh as Cliff chokes at my response. "But aside from that, we're abc, you know? Though, if it makes you uncomfortable you don't have to be around. Cliff and I can keep our time private if you don't want to see it. I won't be offended. I always want you to be comfortable with anything that happens."

Trig raises his hands in front of him and raises his eyebrows. "Oh no, I don't have a problem with it. I was just worried you did. I'm very okay with watching you two together. Like, very okay."

"And participating?" Cliff asks.

"Okay with that too." Trig smiles. "Really just okay with anything involving you two. Except, uh, whatever it was you were doing with that clown. That sounds sketchy."

"Clown?" I look at Cliff with a raised eyebrow.

"Another time, sweetie." He kisses my forehead, and I want to melt. "Trig, go into Crystal's bedroom, in the drawer with her toys there is a bottle of lubrication. Please bring that to me."

"How do you know what's in my drawers?" I ask.

At the same time, Trig says, "Um, okay, I guess," and goes to my room.

"I had a peek while you were gone before I made my way out here. You'll thank me. Though, if you don't like what I propose, you remember what I said."

"I can say no."

"Correct."

Trig comes back over and hands the bottle to Cliff, who sets it on the side table.

"Alright, Trig. We have a wonderful opportunity. The world's most beautiful woman is before us in a state previously unknown to mankind, and if we don't fuck her silly, we'd be complete idiots. If she isn't as wobbly and invisible as a bowl of unflavored gelatin by the time we're done with her, we've lost an incredible opportunity. Get undressed."

I have to admit, I like his plan. Trig seems to as well because he very quickly whips off his white t-shirt and jeans, pulling his boxers off with them, and stands ready.

"Good. Crystal, stand up and face Trig. Trig, kneel before her, and pleasure her with your mouth. I'll use my fingers behind her. She needs to come."

"You're so formal about this," I try to say in a joking voice, but it comes out shaky as Trig buries his face between my thighs and begins to lick my clit.

"I know what works. Fuck, that's so interesting. I can see everything Trig is doing." He pauses as he watches Trig work on me. "Trig, flatten your tongue when you get to that part," Cliff instructs. I have to admit, it's a good instruction.

Cliff inserts one, then two fingers inside me and begins to work in time with Trig. They make a wonderful pair and as Cliff inserts another finger inside me, Trig sucks on my clit, making me moan, feeling my orgasm approaching already.

When it breaks through, Cliff removes his fingers, pausing to instruct Trig once more. "Don't stop," he commands, and I whine at the overwhelming feelings of the continued sensation. Then I hear a bottle pop open and feel cool wetness rubbed on my rear entrance.

"Oh! Um."

"Just my fingers," Cliff soothes. "Relax."

I do as he says and let him carefully, slowly work to stretch my ass as Trig continues. When I look down, I can see Trig's eyes moving between my face and Cliff's fingers and I think about how strange this all must look to them. The thought somehow, that I'm so special and exotic, turns me on even more than I already am and another orgasm creeps up and crashes through me.

"You're ready, sweetie. Trig, carry her to the bedroom, I'll meet you there."

In a moment, Trig and I are lying in the bed facing each other, stroking each other's hair. We kept the light on bright to see every bit of one another. It might not be the most romantic mood lighting, but I get to see every freckle, every scar, and I love it. He has a lot of little scars. Knowing how much of a klutz he is, I'm sure there is an accident behind each of them. I can't wait to hear every story.

In another moment, Cliff hobbles into the room on his crutches. I know better than to offer to help him; he's moving fine, and his pride would be wounded if I made it seem otherwise. He sits on the end of the bed and holds out the crutches, waiting. Trig jumps up and grabs them, setting them against a dresser. It makes me smile how adorably subservient Trig is. I just want to pat him on the head and tell him he's a good boy. Maybe sometime I will.

"Here we are. Crystal, come here, sweetie," Cliff says as he begins taking off his clothes. I lick my lips and do as he says.

I hover my hands over his belt buckle while he is removing his shirts. "May I?"

"You may," he replies with a heated look.

I've never removed a pair of pants as fast in my life.

"Trig, have you ever penetrated a woman anally?" Cliff asks in his no-nonsense way that makes me want to hide.

"Uh, no. Why?" Trig replies from next to Cliff on the edge of the bed.

"Just be slow, careful, and let her relax into it. Take this." Cliff hands Trig the bottle of lubrication. "Use it liberally on her and yourself. Crystal, face me. On my lap. Then we can stop fucking talking. One day I promise you two will be well-trained and we won't need to bother with all of this."

"Yes, Sir." I don't really know what else to say to something like that. Anyway, I'm glad to be done talking and to start the—

I yelp as a cold dribble goes down my backside. Then I remember it's just Trig. Okay. Trig massages the slippery liquid onto me as I straddle Cliff's tattooed thighs.

"Climb onto my cock sweetie. Fill your pretty cunt."

I shiver as I follow Cliff's instruction, groaning as the thick, pierced member enters my slick channel.

"All the way. Take it all the way in. Be a good girl, now," he instructs as I work to fit him all the way inside.

When he's fully seated inside me, we both sigh at the feeling of a perfect fit.

"Lay down with me. Let Trig inside. Such a shame he can't see your perfect, tight ass when he fucks it. Oh well, we'll still watch the cum dripping out of your gaping asshole when he pulls out, right, my sweet little slut?"

Cliff leans forward and bites my nipple. I clench around him as I grit my teeth, trying to hold in my shout. When I collect myself, I reply, "That's right. I want you both fucking me until I'm pouring cum from both holes. Please, Trig, hurry."

"You heard her, Trig. Go on now."

Trig brushes the hair away from my neck and presses himself against my back. He leans close to my ear and whispers, "Tell me if it's too much. Just say, I don't know, pecan pie, and I'll stop."

"Pecan pie?" I ask, confused.

"Yeah," he says a little louder. "Pecan pie is the safe word, Cliff."

"Good boy," Cliff purrs.

Trig hisses and presses harder against me.

"Alright. Okay. I love you, Crystal. Even when I can't see you, you're beautiful."

Before I can process the fact he just declared his love for me, I feel the head of his cock press against my back entrance. I try to breathe evenly, setting my forehead on Cliff's chest. He pushes in just a bit, stretching me enough to make me inhale sharply. Trig pauses to feather me with light kisses along my neck and shoulder.

"You feel so good, Crystal. Let me make you feel amazing." I relax at his sweet words and gentle touches as he pushes in further.

I can feel him pressing against Cliff's cock now. The idea excites me so much I push backward against Trig, wanting him inside me even further now. Trig holds me by my chest, each hand massaging a breast, as he moves his hips forward the last couple of inches. When he's fully inside me I'm panting, my hair sweaty on my brow. I've never felt this full.

"This is beautiful," Cliff says with pure wonder in his voice. I follow his eyes to the occupied space between my legs and see the two cocks inside me, one on top of the other. They're so close they could almost be touching if it weren't for a thin, invisible layer between them.

"Somebody do something," I say with a laugh after everyone stands there and stares for far too long.

"Not a problem," Trig chuckles. He begins to carefully pull his hips backward and slide out of me.

Cliff's eyes are wide as he watches the space between us the entire time. When Trig is almost entirely out of me, he thrusts back inside in one quick push. I moan, high and breathy. That catches Cliff's attention.

"That's it. So hungry for our cocks you're moaning like an animal in heat." Cliff holds onto my hips and thrusts up into me in time with Trig. The feeling is so overwhelming my eyes roll backward like I'm possessed. "My poor little cock-hungry slut. Give her everything, Trig. She's such a good girl, fill her ass with your cum. Let's watch it splatter her sweet insides."

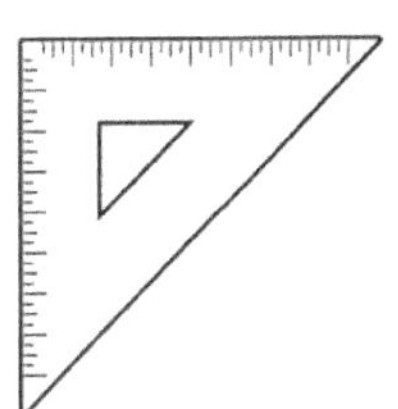

Chapter Twenty-Eight
Cliff

"**Y**es, Sir," he practically scrapes out.

Good. I love watching them when they're barely holding onto control like this. They're both so unlike this outside of these interactions. Watching them this way is intoxicating. Of course, I don't have real control over them, and I wouldn't want to. I only want what they want, and I know they want the same for me. I love them.

"Oh fuck, you look so fucking good through her. I can feel your cock rubbing against mine. Your piercings, Cliff... Holy fuck, Crystal, your ass is so tight. Let me rub your clit, baby. You like that? Shit. I don't know how long I can last." Trig even babbles when he fucks, apparently.

I reach over Crystal and slap my hand over Trig's mouth. "Next time we get a gag for you."

Trig nods vigorously and I can't help but snort. He's going to be such a fun plaything.

Crystal shakes and keens on top of me as Trig rubs her clit between us. It's clear she's about to come. I hold her hips steady and thrust up into her, knowing she's the type to freeze during an intense orgasm and will need me to hold her up. Of course, I'm right. From the bare outline I can see of her, I can tell her mouth opens and her eyes squeeze shut. She stills as Trig and I increase our pace. I can feel my own orgasm approaching, but I try to fend it off. It's important to me that both of my darlings get theirs before I do. Thankfully, Trig isn't far behind Crystal.

"I can't hold back," he rasps out.

"Then don't." I pull his face to mine, and we kiss over Crystal's soft shoulder.

When I feel his body quake I pull away and snap my eyes to the area between Crystal's thighs. I don't want to miss this.

Trig's movements falter and soon a stream of cum shoots into Crystal, splattering inside her. It's the strangest, but somehow the hottest, fucking thing I've ever seen.

"Good boy," is all I can say before my own orgasm begins.

My cum splashes Crystal's vagina, smearing against the walls as I push and pull in and out of her. My cum and Trig's is close, so close, but separate. We both finally lay still, panting and softening inside our central partner.

"You did so well, Crystal." I rub her back with one hand and softly scratch her scalp with the other. "I've never felt something so wonderful. I love you so much."

I kiss Crystal on her temple and smile when Trig leans over her and kisses her in the same spot. He scoots his body down to the floor so that he's sitting with his back to the chair and looks up at both of us with a mischievous grin. I get ready for some kind of bullshit.

Of course, Trig opens his mouth and says, "I love you too, Crystal. You know, I can't wait until you reopen the restaurant. You have the best cream pies."

Crystal sits up and glares at him. "You butt-hole," she snaps.

I get prepared to stop a fight between them. *This is not how I wanted this evening to end.* Instead, Crystal smiles.

"I was going to make that joke. I can't believe you got there first." She pouts.

"You snooze, you lose."

"You're both children. I retract all of my previous praise," I grumble.

Internally, however, I'm beaming in delight. *Two. I have two of them.* How is that possible for someone like me? Well, whatever god blessed me deserves thanks and not the insult of my questioning. I'll accept the gift I've been given.

Trig and Crystal hold one another on the floor, nose to nose. Trig reaches to smooth her hair but misses his target, hand flailing around behind her before finding it. Crystal laughs with a snort that makes Trig laugh in response. Soon enough they're both giggling and rolling around on the floor. They're attempting a tickle fight, but Crystal wins easily with her ability to locate Trig's body parts far more easily than he can hers. Of course, he abuses the ability to see our cum still in her body to find her more than once, which seems to be driving her insane.

"Okay, enough cum-spotting. I'm taking a shower and then getting dressed," Crystal announces before taking off toward the bathroom.

"Boo! Hiss!" Trig calls after her, thumbs down.

"It's alright Trig. You'll need a shower next anyway. Lay with me for now. Talk to me. How are you feeling?" I ask.

"I'm good. Great, actually," he replies as he crawls into the bed next to me. "Probably never felt this good. Only thing that would be better is if we knew for sure Crystal was going to return to normal. It's kind of scary right now even though we're pretty sure she'll be fine. Oh, and I'm still worried about your leg. That's a bummer."

"My leg is fine. It will heal soon enough. As for Crystal, I too am worried but also believe she'll be fine. Trig, I'm so incredibly happy to have her. You as well. What a wonderful life this will be." Letting myself be vulnerable like this will take some getting used to but I could come to like it.

"It's really gonna be great. So, by the way, are we going to all live together right away? Or is that moving too fast? Because you two have land connected. It only seems natural to just have the two of you stay here, but the question is do we keep both houses or rebuild one big one? We definitely shouldn't live in mine. It's small, and oh boy, is it messy. Don't worry though, I promise to keep our mutual home clean. I won't—"

"Trig, please, stop." I run a hand across my eyes. This man is going to give me many headaches. "Let's not worry about that for now."

"Okay, but I hope my cat gets along with her dog. Pytha is an indoor cat and has only ever lived alone."

"You named your cat after Pythagoras? Who was an influence on Plato, the name of Crystal's dog?" I ask with my eyebrow raised.

"Yeah! Isn't that cool?" He smiles. His hair is poking up every which way and his cheeks are still flushed.

"You're both nerds."

"Aww man," Crystal says from the doorway, apparently having overhead that last bit of conversation. "Don't lump me in with him."

"No way. You're stuck with me now, nerderino," Trig tosses a pillow at Crystal as she pulls a cotton nightgown over her head.

"*Oof.* Freaking hell. I just got called a nerderino and somehow, I still love you. This is dumb." Crystal leaps onto the bed and flops between Trig and me. "Eh, I could get used to it, I guess. The two hot naked guys in my bed thing *is* pretty nice."

"You deserve everything nice in the world, Crystal. You're nothing but kind. Now, we need some rest and when we wake up, we'll see if the world will return the kindness you've given to it."

Chapter Twenty-Nine
Cliff

The scent of the air is taunting me, reminding me of my failure to be on time. Normally, I take my lunch at eleven a.m. exactly. I like to be punctual. Today, however, I needed to go home and shower after a particularly dirty display piece was sent to the museum. Now it's after twelve and the mornings-only café where I eat each day is closed. *Damn.*

I stand in front of the closed café, still able to smell the bacon sandwiches I order every day and watch the light traffic on Main Street.

I shuffle nervously in place, propped on the cane I use these days after the accident, as I look around at the people going about their day. The weather today is unseasonably cool for summer, so there are plenty of people out and about. Mothers walk their small children in strollers. Old men sit on benches arguing about local politics. A beautiful woman with icy blonde hair hangs a sign in a shop window.

I've seen that woman many times before. Every night she's in my bed, along with our other lover. Once a month, she's invisible at night, but she's back to normal by morning.

The woman steps back, placing her hands on her wide hips, and looks up at the sign to check her work. She readjusts it just slightly and looks over it once more. With a satisfied nod, she steps away and walks inside the brick building.

**Crystal's Pies
Now Open Late**

The sign sparkles in glittering rainbow letters. Pie. *Hmm.* Not the healthiest lunch but it's good and I'm hungry.

My anxiety over any unexpected change doesn't want me dining there.

But you know who it is. It's a safe place. There's love there.

And did you see how beautiful she was?

My libido chimes in as it usually does nowadays. *Why don't you go and get a taste of her pie?*

A man with sandy brown hair trips over a rock and stumbles, catching himself on a bike rack outside the shop. I shake my head. *Someone needs to keep that man alive.*

That decides it. I cross the street and head toward the shop.

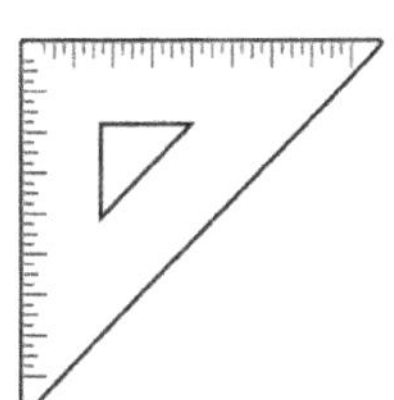

Bonus Epilogue
Cliff

"Trig!"

The door slams shut behind me. I stand in the entryway to Trig's house, completely in shock. A tabby cat looks up at me from atop a pile of philosophy books, which are stacked on the floor next to a coffee table littered with notebooks and coffee cups. The whole place is a goddamn mess.

"Trig! Damn it, where are you?" I shout into the house as I walk farther in.

I scoot several cat toys out of the way with my cane as I travel the living room, heading toward upbeat music. When I make it across that hell hole, I turn a corner into a kitchen to find Trig doing dishes, swaying to a calypso beat. At first, he startles when I tap his leg with my cane, but then smiles when he sees it's only me.

"Hi Cliff! You're early! I would have been outside waiting for you in an hour. Wait, it is early, right? I lose track of time sometimes." Trig scratches his head with one wet hand, leaving soap bubbles in his hair.

"I am early, yes. I want to spend a moment alone with you before we go to the event tonight. Just to check in. We've been so busy the last few days we haven't gotten much time alone." I can't help it; I'm addicted to him.

"Aww, you missed me. That's so sweet," Trig says as he attempts to hug me. I snap my cane up between us.

"You and Crystal with the *sweet* thing. Terrible. Either way I'm certainly in no *sweet* mood after seeing this wreck of a house. If we're all going to cohabitate at some point you're going to have to learn to clean up."

"I know, I know. It just gets overwhelming. And you know, it's not even that bad compared to how it used to be. There's no garbage or anything around! And I'm doing the dishes! Except the coffee cups. I still need to do those. But I'll get to them. I mean, really, the mess is most-ly books and laundry. A few good bookshelves and—"

"Trig, please, the babbling." I tug on the wrinkly collar of his shirt. "You're not even dressed for tonight, speaking of laundry. Just finish this later, we have places to be."

"Uh, okay I guess." He pulls the drain in the sink and rinses his hands, wiping them dry on his pants. The hand towel is *right there*, for fuck's sake. *Sigh.*

I follow Trig as he walks to his room to change. When we get there, I'm frozen at the door. Dirty laundry. Everywhere. Why does a man even need these many clothes? And why must they be on the floor? I shake my head as he tosses his socks toward the hamper but misses.

"Enough. The dirty laundry. Pick it up," I bark the order at him. He jumps at the sound of my voice.

"Um, we don't have time."

"Then we'll be late."

To my surprise a smile appears on Trig's face, his adorably crooked tooth making an appear-ance.

"This is just like when we were young," he says before picking up a t-shirt and tossing it into the hamper. "Except now I know why I feel kind of funny when you yell at me."

I clear my throat and adjust my collar, under which I have begun to grow warm. "Yes. Well. Unlike when we were young, I'm not cleaning it for you. So."

I point my cane at the mess on the floor and return to my position monitoring his cleaning up. Trig offers me a salute, to which I roll my eyes. Then he begins to pick up the mess.

He quickly gets into a rhythm and doesn't take nearly as long as I thought he would to finish picking up. When he tosses the last sock into a laundry basket next to the hamper, he turns to me with a grin, dusting off his hands.

"All done. Time to get dressed and go," he cheerily says. I shake my head.

"No. I said all of the dirty laundry."

He follows my eyes as my gaze drags from the hem of his shirt, where there is a small ink stain, to the first button, which has some sort of pink crust on it. Trig's cheeks flush as he tries to brush off the mess.

"I was eating a cupcake. Pink frosting. Crystal's experimenting."

"Mmhmm. Take it off." I point to the laundry basket.

His throat bobs as he swallows and unbuttons the top button. "Yes, Sir."

Fuck, I love him.

The shirt is soon in the basket as well as his pants. With a nod of my head to his boxers he takes those off as well. I smirk at the sight of the rock-hard length of him. It seems he does get a *funny feeling*. I fold my jacket and set it carefully on the dresser. When I roll up my white shirt sleeves, I see Trig's already pink cheeks grow red.

"Did you shower already, Trig?"

"Uh, yes. Yes, this morning." He fumbles nervously over his words.

His hair is as incredibly soft as always between my fingers when I bring the side of his face against mine. I drag my nose down his neck, inhaling his scent. Inexpensive, no-nonsense soap, made for sensitive skin. The same as always.

"Good. Undress me and fold my clothes nicely. I want to make sure you can do it properly." I loosen my tie and wait.

"And then what?" His hands shake as he unbuttons my shirt.

I lean in close to his ear and let the words rumble from my chest, "I'm going to fuck you, Trig."

He nods quickly several times as he hurries to finish removing my button-down, followed by my undershirt. When he reveals the triangle tattoo underneath, he pauses to trace his fingers along its sides, as he always does, before moving onto my belt. I kick off my own shoes but let him line them up neatly next to the door, where I prop my cane next to them.

"Tell me, Trig," I begin as I walk toward him, forcing him to walk backward, "what would best help you with keeping your spaces clean? Reward or punishment?"

"I, uh, I don't know," he stutters out before flopping down onto his bed, nowhere else to go. "Wish I knew."

"Perhaps we should find out. What do you think?"

Leaning over him now, hands on either side of his shoulders, I can see the pulse beating frantically in his jugular. I want to tear it out with my teeth.

"I just...I think..." His eyes dart between us just briefly before I feel his hand wrap around my cock. "Whatever you want. That's what I think."

Stifling a groan, I reluctantly remove Trig's hand from my aching member. I thread my other hand through the back of his hair, lifting him as if for a kiss, before yanking his hair to the side at the last moment, pressing my lips against his ear.

"Punishment it is."

With some reluctance, I release Trig, setting him on the mattress chest down, face to the side. Slowly, so as not to bother my leg, I step to the dresser and grab my belt from atop the neatly folded pile of clothes. When I return to Trig, I take a moment to admire his lithe form, and flawless skin, before crouching behind his prone figure.

"The wonderful thing about keeping items where they belong is that it's easy to find them when you need them. For example, I was able to find this belt right away. I didn't need to search around for it on the floor. Arms behind your back." Trig follows my instructions and puts his arms behind his back, wrists held together. "Mmm, very good at following instructions. Still, so bad at sticking to rules when left to your own devices."

"Please. I want to touch you. You know how much I want to touch you," Trig begs.

"*Tsk.* You have to earn that right, to be my little plaything. Right now, you're just a naughty whore who needs to learn a lesson."

"I'll do anything. I'll suck your cock. Whatever you want. Just let me touch you." He's breathless now. Desperate. But he's not saying our safe word, the little scamp.

"You're lucky I don't gag you. Fortunately for you, I love to hear you when I fuck your tight ass." *Oh, fuck* I don't know how much longer I can put off taking my own pleasure. I've never had this problem in my life but with Crystal and Trig, it's as if I can't resist being inside them as soon as the chance is offered. It's paradise.

"Then please fuck me. Punish me with your huge cock. I promise I'll be better." He arches against me, and I can no longer stifle the moan that has been trying to escape.

"Well, since you asked so nicely," I say, my voice coming from low in my chest, my breath already heavy.

I nearly tear open the drawer to the small nightstand next to me and pull out the bottle of lube I know is there. Ripping the cap off with my teeth, I pull Trig up against me and hold him carefully by the throat. My other hand massages the slippery substance onto my already dripping cock and into his sweet asshole. I run my hand up and down his throat, the threat alone enough to make him shake.

"You're so tight, Trig. Relax for me. Be a good whore so I can fuck you right. You need this big cock inside you, so you won't ever forget the feeling of me completely wrecking you. You'll always have that reminder to be a good boy, won't you, my little fuck toy? Don't you want to be good for me?" I run the tip of my cock along his crack in a tease, making him whine.

"Yes, Sir. I want to be good."

"So, relax."

Trig takes a few calming breaths and soon I'm able to slide a few fingers inside him. Not long after I press my cock against his asshole and push until I pass the tight ring of muscle. Trig moans and writhes against me. I twitch and grit my teeth every time one of my piercings enters him. The first entrance of our lovemaking is always a torturous pleasure for us. When I make it fully inside, stretching him wide, hitting him deep with my pierced cock, we're both quiet for a moment. Our heavy breathing is the only sound in the room until I lean into Trig and ask what I always do, even if he gets a little annoyed that it breaks the mood.

"Are you okay?"

"I'm fine, Cliff. Back to the pounding, please," he laughs in a strained tone.

Knowing he's alright, I can go back to the fun.

I slowly slide out of him, almost all of the way, then force my way back in. Thus begins the brutal pounding Trig needs.

I shove his face onto the mattress so that his head is turned to the side, holding him down with a grip on his hair. My other arm pulls back only to slam forward, spanking Trig's ass as I pound into it. The way he cries out is beautiful. I spank him again.

I grab both of his hips and thrust into him as deep as I can. Trig presses his face into the mattress and shouts long and loud into the soft bedding. That's enough to push me over the edge, even though I want to stay inside him forever. I spill my cum inside him, groaning deeply as I finish hard. When I pull out, my cum dribbles out of him and down his thighs. It's a beautiful sight.

"Have you learned your lesson?"

I sit on the edge of the bed and lift Trig onto my lap. His hair is a staticky mess that makes him look somehow even more handsome than usual. I smooth it down with my fingers, softly scratching his scalp.

"Yes, I have. I'll be much better at keeping things tidy, I promise." He sounds sleepy like he always does after we make love.

"Very good." I undo the belt from his wrists. Immediately, he puts his arms in front of himself and rubs his wrists with a sigh. "I think you've been a very good boy. You've followed my instructions, and you took my cock so well. I think you may even deserve to come. Do you think you deserve to come, little plaything?"

"If you think I do then yes, please," he breathes out.

"Then lay down. I'll assist you. Remember Trig, I'll always be here for you when you need me. I love you." I stroke his soft cheek, cleanly shaven for the day, and he smiles before nuzzling into my shoulder. Then, he lies down on his back, hands folded on his stomach.

People might believe I was submissive in this position. Those people would be very wrong. This is simply a reward for good behavior.

I straddle Trig's thighs and kiss his flat stomach. I can't help but run my fingers along his Adonis belt. He sighs happily, completely relaxed. Good. When I take his cock into my hand he lifts his hips, his mouth dropping open.

"Stay still," I admonish him. He knows better. Trig nods and settles back onto the mattress.

Then I drop and take him into my mouth. He has a perfect cock. Big, but not overly large. Wonderfully shaped. And he tastes fantastic. I'm very good at this and it doesn't take long before Trig comes with a long moan of my name. *Perfect.*

I crawl up to meet him at the top of the bed then wrap my arms around him. His cheeks are flushed as if he's been on a winter walk, and he's looking at me as if I've performed a miracle.

"I love you," he whispers.

"I love you too, my very good boy," I whisper back.

"*Mrow*," says Pytha as she jumps onto the bed and lays between us. I frown at her but Trig scratches between her ears, making her purr. Hmm. I suppose if she makes Trig happy, I'll tolerate her. The cat is...cute, I guess. I use one finger to pet the cat along its back briefly before pulling back. *There.* I made an effort.

"I need to shower again before we go to that geology event. I think I got a little musky there," Trig admits.

"Fuck the event. The rest of the department can handle it. I do everything every day. Today I'm staying in and helping my partner clean his disgusting house, and when our other partner finishes her work, we're all going to have filthy sex on the clean floors. I don't have time for mingling and cocktails."

Trig sits up and stares at me as if I've grown a second head.

"What? You're not the only one who can change," I grumble. We look at each other, him with eyebrows raised, another moment before we both start laughing.

"I love you so much, Cliff. For someone with such strict routines, I really never know what to expect from you. You keep me on my toes. Okay, I'll be right back, I have to use the restroom." He stands up and begins to walk to the door before turning back to me. "Hey wait. Are we really going to have to clean until Crystal gets off work? That's hours from now."

"Yes, we are." I nod.

"So that means the filthy group sex on the clean floors too then?" He smiles in that boyish way that makes him look young again.

"Absolutely. But only if they're clean."

"I'll get my mop as soon as I get out of the restroom. If I can find the mop." He salutes me and takes off out of the door. I pet the cat with one finger, loving her as best I can because Trig loves her.

Because I love him.

Dedication

This book is dedicated to Cassie, Latrexa, Shannon, Tee, Courtney, and Alijay. Without all of you I wouldn't have been able to make this book a success.

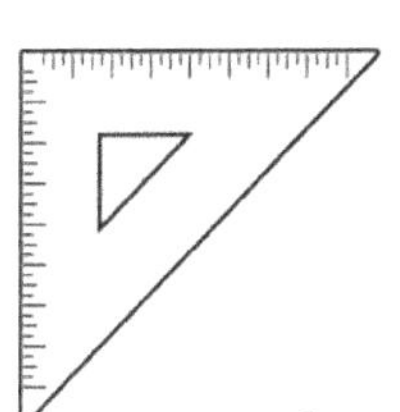

Also From Sylvia Morrow

R ead below for more on *Stuffed*, a living pillow romance, from Sylvia Morrow.

***

She thought she'd never be able to find a lover, but he's been in her bed for years.

Anime obsessed Anne might be a fictophiliac, or she might just hate touch so much she'll never have sex. She doesn't really care about the difference as long as she has her favorite pillow to grind against when she needs physical relief.

Anne's favorite pillow is more than just a feather-filled cotton sack--he's alive but no one knows it. Hot, pulsing magic weaves between his fibers each time she touches him. All he wants is to be the man Anne needs.

Soft. Moldable. And ready to cater to her every desire.

But when he has enough magic to become a man, will Anne accept his eager touch? Can flesh and fabric come together in erotic bliss? Will more than one of them end up fully stuffed?

Stuffed is for adult readers only. It is the first in a three-book series but can be read stand-alone. You can find *Stuffed* on Amazon on eBook and Kindle Unlimited, on audiobook on iTunes, Amazon, and Audible, and on paperback in many different places (just ask your local store or library, they might even have it!) *Repleta*, the Spanish eBook translation, is sold wide and in many libraries already.

www.ingramcontent.com/pod-product-compliance
Lightning Source LLC
Chambersburg PA
CBHW060403310726
48976CB00003B/928